D0813539

WINTERFIRE

Lois Faye Dyer

A KISMET™ Romance

 METEOR PUBLISHING CORPORATION
Bensalem, Pennsylvania

KISMET™ is a trademark of Meteor Publishing Corporation

Copyright © 1990 Lois Faye Dyer
Cover art copyright © 1990 Alex Zwarenstein

All rights reserved.

No part of this book may be reproduced, stored in a retrieval system, or transmitted in any form, by any means, including mechanical, electronic, photocopying, recording or otherwise, without prior written permission of the publisher, Meteor Publishing Corporation, 3369 Progress Drive, Bensalem, PA 19020.

First Printing July 1990.

ISBN: 1-878702-03-3.

All the characters in this book are ficticious. Any resemblance to actual persons, living or dead, is purely coincidental.

Printed in the United States of America.

For my husband, Bud, for all the reasons that only he knows.

You and I, we chose the road less travelled by,
And that has made all the difference.

LOIS FAYE DYER

Lois Faye Dyer ended a career as a paralegal and Superior Court Clerk to fulfill a lifelong dream to write. She lives on Washington State's beautiful Puget Sound, with her husband, two children, and their erascible parrot, Dylan. When she's not involved in writing, she enjoys long walks on the beach with her husband, watching musical and western movies from the 1940's and 1950's and, most of all, indulging her passionate addiction to reading.

ONE

"Oh no!"

The rental car's engine spluttered and coughed—again! The little red Mazda seemed sturdy enough when Ashley rented it at the Boise airport, but for the last forty miles it had choked and gasped with alarming frequency.

"Just a few more miles." She prayed aloud with heartfelt fervor. "Please! It can't be that much farther to Antelope!"

The road she traveled on twisted and wound through the hills and valleys of Idaho ranchland. After a brief look at the road map, provided by the clerk at the car rental agency, Ashley had estimated that the drive from the airport to her friend's ranch outside Antelope, Idaho, would take her two hours at most. But the time had stretched into three hours, and now four. She shot an anxious glance at the diamond-studded face of her wristwatch.

"Ten o'clock already," she murmured into the stillness of the car. The only response was the whir of the heater working industriously to keep the frigid air outside at bay.

Her slim fingers sifted through her hair and pushed the thick silken mane away from her face. The time difference between Idaho and New York City was three hours and her tired body was aching, telling her that it was one o'clock in the morning and far past her bedtime. She'd left her warm bed in Manhattan at four A.M. because the photographer for *Vogue* wanted to catch the sunrise. Ashley knew the fantasy furs contrasted against the gritty realism of the East River waterfront would make stunning photographs, but that didn't help her tired body right now. She badly needed a bed and at least twelve hours of sleep.

Her soft mouth tightened, as she remembered the final argument with her aunt after the photo session. Magda Tierney used every persuasive argument she knew to make Ashley cancel this Christmas vacation in Idaho, but for once Ashley held firm and refused to give in. Lately, the silken chains of loyalty that bound Ashley to her aunt were chafing even more than usual. A deep-seated, restless boredom with her life as one of the world's top fashion models was growing stronger daily. At twenty-four, she had already been working in the business for sixteen years. Her aunt had found Ashley employment as a child model when she was only eight years old, and still shell-shocked from the death of her parents in a fiery automobile crash and the appointment of Magda, her father's sister, as her guardian. Aunt Magda's soft, blonde feminine facade hid a will of iron and a discerning eye for both fashion and finances, not to mention a streak of hardboiled practicality.

Ashley hated upsetting her aunt; Magda was the only family she had left. Still, she couldn't continue living her life as Magda saw fit. Not when it was patently unfulfilling. Ashley's problem was how to convince Magda that she had no desire to pursue the extremely lucrative career that her aunt had worked so hard for her to achieve.

Ashley sighed heavily. It wasn't going to be easy. She needed this time away from her aunt and the city to do some serious thinking about the direction her life was moving in. She might just decide to alter that direction forever. She thought briefly of the sketches packed in her bag, brought along to demonstrate to Joanne her plan to illustrate children's books, and put to use both her natural talent and the college degree she had stubbornly fought Magda to obtain. Bouncing ideas off Joanne was something she had often done when the two of them had shared a tiny dormitory room at college. She needed to discuss this latest plan with her eminently practical friend. Joanne never hesitated to tell her if any of her ideas were crazy.

Ashley scanned the road ahead anxiously. The night was dark, the moon only a narrow sickle that cast its silver light down over the black ribbon of highway. The blacktop stretched ahead and wound around the pine-dotted, snow-covered side of a mountain. She hadn't passed another vehicle for miles and felt very alone in the empty, silent wilderness. Above her, glittering stars hung suspended from the vaulted dome of the black sky and the moon's silver rays only added to her sense of isolation.

The little car hiccupped and sputtered once again and Ashley's finger tightened apprehensively on the steering wheel.

Damn, I'm tired! J.D. McCullough leaned denim-clad elbows on the polished surface of the Blue Cougar's bar and stared moodily into the frothy surface of his beer. He ignored the whiskey-rough voice of Willie Nelson growling from the neon-lit jukebox and the friendly wrangling of the three cowboys playing pool in the back of the saloon. A blue haze of cigarette and cigar smoke hung in the low-ceilinged room. J.D.'s eyes narrowed to shield his midnight irises—the only outward sign that he was aware of his surroundings.

Bone-weary tired. Not only from the long day, which began by chasing the gelding and two mares that broke through a fence in the home pasture and strayed into the Bear Creek Foothills sometime before dawn. An odd restlessness rode him hard, undermining the satisfaction of a job well done which he usually felt after long hours in the saddle chasing steers or horses, or riding the fence lines looking for breaks, or any one of a dozen other physically demanding chores necessary on the ranch.

He didn't exactly enjoy the bookkeeping that went hand in hand with owning and running the biggest ranch in Idaho, but he never avoided it either. For some reason he couldn't define, he hadn't wanted to go home to the silent ranch house tonight. He'd stopped in at the Blue Cougar for a beer because he didn't want to go home to the stack of book work spread across the scarred oak desk where McCulloughs had been doing the ranch books since the 1800s. J.D. was a loner and he couldn't understand his sudden reluctance to be alone.

He shifted on the bar stool's red-vinyl seat, one booted foot planted solidly on the floor and the other heel hooked over the scarred brass rail. He tilted the long-necked beer bottle, his tanned throat muscles moving rhythmically as he swallowed.

His gaze drifted past the rim of the bottle to the mirror backing the bar and he stopped swallowing, his lean fingers freezing the glass at his lips. His black stare was riveted by the mirror's reflection of a woman stepping through the doorway, hesitating on the threshold as she surveyed the smoky saloon and its male occupants.

Slowly, painfully, J.D.'s muscles unclenched and his hand returned the bottle to the polished bar where its moisture beaded bottom stamped another damp ring. His black brows lifted over night-dark eyes; his gaze moving over the reflection with slow amazement.

What the hell is someone like her doing in Antelope, Idaho?

Everything about the woman in the doorway fairly screamed big city and money. A thick mane of sable hair, shot with streaks of gold, flowed off her face and fell to her shoulders. It lay like dark silk against the upturned collar of a full-length dark mink coat. Slim fingers held the heavy coat together. What J.D. could see of the body underneath was curved in all the right places. The legs were slim and shapely, a thin gold bracelet circling one slender ankle above Italian-shod feet.

J.D. registered all of her in one slow, absorbing glance and moved back to focus on her face. He found wide-spaced eyes, which even at this distance gleamed gold beneath thick, black lashes, and a fine-boned nose above a mouth that was soft and lush and pink. Dark brows winged above those gold eyes. *Lioness' eyes*, J.D. thought. Although right now, with that uncertain air, she looked more like a kitten than a lioness.

Ashley hesitated in the doorway of the saloon.

The room was blue with cigarette smoke and a country-western singer growled out of the jukebox in the corner. There were at least twenty men at the bar and scattered among the round tables. They all turned and stared at her with open curiosity. Three cowboys playing pool in the back stopped and leaned on their wooden cues to stare.

This is worse than modeling lingerie with twenty photographer's assistants looking on!

A flush moved up her throat and burnt across her cheeks. Ashley had never conquered her innate shyness, but she had learned to hide it behind a distancing calm. Falling back on a trick that she'd learned early in her career to calm the swooping and diving stomach butterflies, she took a deep breath, held it, and walked across the silent room to the mirror-backed bar, ignoring the stares from the tables. The bartender watched her, with a dumfounded, bemused look on his face.

"Oh, my gawd!" Nate Tucker whispered reverently, his Adam's apple bobbing jerkily in his skinny throat. "Would you look at that!"

"Damn!" Ed Thorson's bloodshot blue eyes were wide with astonishment. One ham-size fist shoved his beat-up Stetson back off his forehead, revealing a thatch of blonde hair above the tan line. "Ain't she somethin'!"

J.D. ran a thoughtful hand over the day's growth of black stubble shadowing his jaw and silently agreed. *She was somethin', all right*. His forefinger unconsciously stroked down the thin scar that ran from temple to jaw, and the silent reminder of the damage done by another beautiful woman snapped him back to reality.

His black eyes turned cold and hard. He had good cause to dislike beautiful women, especially those that loved riches. He tilted the beer bottle again and kept his back to the room.

"Excuse me," the husky, low-pitched tone carried easily across the suddenly quiet bar. "I wonder if you have a phone I could use? My car broke down and I need to call a friend."

"Sure thing, lady," bartender Al Davis grinned fatuously. "Right here."

He lifted the Blue Cougar's phone from the ledge next to the beer taps and clapped it down on the bar with a flourish.

Ashley smiled her thanks at him. His foolish grin seemed likely to become a permanent part of his face.

Perfectly manicured nails tipped the fingers that dialled the phone. J.D. pretended not to notice the absence of a ring on her left hand.

The phone rang and rang, and rang some more. Ashley counted fifteen rings before she sighed and gave up.

She dropped the receiver back into its cradle and looked up to find the bartender watching her with open, unabashed curiosity.

"Your friend not home?"

"No—no, I'm afraid not," perfect white teeth worried the soft curve of her bottom lip for a long moment. "Is there a taxi in town?"

"Nope," Al shook his head and waved one big paw in a vague southerly direction. "Closest taxi is in Boise and that's a mighty long way from here."

Great! Just great! Ashley groaned silently. *Would nothing go right today? So far, I'm batting a thousand!*

" 'Scuse me, ma'am."

Ashley half-turned to find a muscled blond giant at her elbow.

"I'd be happy to give you a lift, ma'am." The blue eyes in the youth's tanned, handsome face were eager, expectant, and frankly admiring as their gaze ran over her fur-wrapped body.

"Now hold on a minute, Cole." A tall lanky cowboy with a sunburnt face and grass-green eyes dropped a heavy hand on the younger man's broad shoulder. "I reckon I'll give the little lady a lift."

"No, you won't," Ed Thorson protested vehemently. "I will." He shoved the other two aside and pulled his Stetson off to hold it in front of him. "Just where is it you want to go, ma'am?"

Ashley shoved her hands deep in the pockets of the heavy coat and smiled cautiously at the semi-circle of faces in front of her. For the first time since crossing the threshold, she realized that she was the one and only woman in the room.

"I'm visiting Joanne Kleeman and her husband Blake—do you know them?"

"Why sure I do!" chorused the semicircle which had swelled to fifteen men—all ages, shapes, and sizes.

"I'll take you out to the Kleeman ranch myself, ma'am!" Ed Thorson said firmly, smiling expansively down at her.

"No, you won't, you big, dumb Norwegian," Cole declared hotly, "because I'm going to!"

"Shut up, kid," Nate's green eyes dismissed the younger man. "You don't have to worry about Ed taking her, 'cause I will."

"No, you're not, I am!"

"Like hell, you are! I am!"

"I'm driving her!"

Ashley took a cautious, unobtrusive step backward and was brought up short by the feel of the bar's edge against her back.

A brawl was about to break out in front of her bewildered eyes. The men were squaring off, some even pushing and shoving each other. She had the sinking feeling that she was going to be caught in the middle of flying fists at any moment.

J.D. heard, with mixed feelings, her husky voice identify his neighbors, the Kleemans. He was reluctant to get involved in what was shaping-up to be an all-out fight and not too keen on helping the woman either. On the other hand, Joanne Kleeman and he had grown up together—she was one of the few women he could tolerate.

He got off the barstool and stepped away from the bar.

"I'll take the lady to the Bar K."

His deep drawl held a core of steel edged with finality, and it stopped the arguing men in mid-sentence and brought them all turning to face him.

Ashley's hair swung in a dark fan against the fur covering her shoulders. Her gold gaze searched for the owner of the deep voice and clashed with unrelenting black eyes.

"The Kleemans are my neighbors, ma'am." The deep voice held none of the male eagerness of the other patrons. Its very indifference reassured Ashley. The sight of him, though, did just the opposite.

This man is definitely part of the wild west Aunt Magda lectured me about, she thought. He was tall, over six feet, and broad-shouldered. A faded blue-denim Levi jacket lined with sheepskin stretched over the width of his shoulders. Equally faded blue jeans, soft and white in places from many washings, fit like a second skin over muscled thighs and long calves. Scuffed black cowboy boots covered his feet. A battered black Stetson was pushed back off his forehead to reveal thick black hair. His face was craggy and could have been called handsome except for the thin white scar that ran from temple to jaw on his left cheek. The thin white line was stark against a day's growth of black beard that roughened his jaw and accentuated the tough outlaw appearance of the man.

His eyes were such a deep brown that they appeared black, the eyelashes thick and long. On a less aggressively masculine man, they would have looked effeminate. As Ashley continued to stare wordlessly, one black brow arched inquisitively.

"Are you ready?"

The deep voice jolted her from her absorption and she glanced around the bar.

Before she could force her vocal cords to work, Nate broke in.

"Aw, come on, J.D., let me take her."

"She's a friend of Joanne's, Nate," the slow drawl allowed for no argument. "I'll run her by the ranch."

J.D. moved toward Ashley and halted in front of her, waiting. Ashley searched the hard lines of the handsome face. In New York, she wouldn't have considered accepting a ride from a man whose name she didn't even know. But this was Joanne's hometown and when the tall, tough-looking cowboy claimed to be Joanne's neighbor, no one disputed his word. And despite his rough, desperado appearance, there was something about him that touched off an instant chord of trust, deep in Ashley.

She held out her hand.

"My name is Ashley Tierney—and you are—?"

J.D.'s calloused palm enveloped her much smaller, softer hand.

"J.D. McCullough."

Relief flooded through Ashley. Joanne had talked

about her neighbor J.D. McCullough dozens, maybe hundreds of times. After sharing a college dorm room with Joanne for four years, J.D. and the other residents of Antelope were as familiar to Ashley as if they were her own family and friends. The orphaned Ashley had absorbed the homey tales of Joanne's hometown with an eagerness intensified by her own lonely existence.

She smiled brilliantly up into the dark face above her.

"I feel like I already know you, Mr. McCullough. Joanne speaks of you so often."

J.D. felt as if the sun had broken into the room and smiled at him. He stifled the quick burst of pleasure that warmed him and wondered briefly what Joanne had told her about him.

"Just J.D. is fine."

"Just Ashley is fine, too."

She slid her arm into the crook of his, oblivious to the collective hiss of indrawn breaths from the surrounding men.

J.D. ignored the dumbstruck cowboys. Not a muscle moved over his dark features as he stared down into Ashley's upturned face.

Women in Antelope generally left J.D. alone. And nobody touched him without chancing a cold, scathing remark that could literally strip skin off their soft hide. Although few women had the temerity to approach him, none failed to admire his broad-shouldered, slim-hipped build. Outlaws always appealed to women, the very danger of his attraction made the appeal stronger.

J.D. couldn't have told anyone why he didn't shrug off the fingers that closed gently over his bicep. He did know that he felt the soft touch through denim, sheepskin, and cotton as if it were skin on skin. Warm woman against male. It burned and sent waves of heat radiating up his arm and tingling down to his fingers.

Maybe it was her touch? Maybe it was the complete trust in the gold kitten eyes that smiled up into his? Maybe it was because her gold gaze didn't flinch away from the scar marring the dark skin of his cheek? Whatever it was, J.D. tolerated her hand on him without comment.

Ashley continued to smile at him, completely oblivious that she had just scaled an unclimbable mountain.

"My rental car broke down three blocks from here," she explained. "Do you think we could pick up my luggage before you take me to Joanne's?"

"Sure," J.D. growled. "No problem."

The saloon's occupants watched the elegant woman and the rough cowboy cross the room and disappear into the dark night. Astonishment kept the garrulous patrons silent.

TWO

The Blue Cougar's heavy wooden door swung shut behind the tall cowboy and slender woman, closing off the saloon's stunned patrons.

Ashley shivered and pulled her collar higher against the cold night air.

J.D. felt the involuntary tightening of her fingers on his arm and glanced down at her.

"Cold?"

Her gaze lifted to meet his and she nodded.

"Yes." She dropped her gaze to the icy sidewalk and snuggled deeper into the fur of her collar. "A little. Is it very far to Joanne's ranch?"

"No, about ten miles." J.D. halted at the edge of the sidewalk where snowplows had banked snow a foot high against the curb. He gestured to a

21

four-wheel drive pickup, its silver paint splattered with a mixture of dirt and snow. "This is my rig."

His dark gaze swept swiftly over her and fastened on the Italian pumps on her feet. The supple black leather was already stained with the snow she'd been unable to avoid on her walk from the stalled car to the Blue Cougar.

"Lady, you're lucky that car of yours broke down only three blocks away. If you'd had to hike very far in those shoes, you'd never have made it to Antelope."

"I know, I—oh!" Ashley's explanation was cut off sharply when J.D. bent and slid one arm under her knees, the other across her back, and swung her off her feet.

Ashley grabbed his jacket and held on. Startled gold eyes met unreadable black.

"No sense in getting your feet any wetter." J.D. answered the unvoiced question in her eyes with calm assurance.

"Oh," she managed. Cradled in his arms and held snug against his chest, Ashley felt a strange sense of safety mixed with an odd breathlessness. Her delicate nostrils flared, inhaling his scent. It was a mix of soap, leather, horse—and pure male. She felt a deep satisfaction that he smelled nothing at all like the cologned, three-piece-suited Madison Avenue men Magda had been urging on her in the last few months.

J.D. was having his own problems dealing with

his reaction to the woman in his arms. When he swept her up, it had been a purely sensible action on his part. She wasn't dressed for the Idaho winter. But once he held her, a surge of pure male possessiveness hit him like a tidal wave. She fit as if she were made for his arms—and she felt damned good. The backs of her silk-clad legs were warm where they bent against the back of his hand, and even through the thickness of the fur coat he could tell her body was curved generously. Each breath he took drew in her scent, a combination of woman and perfume, spicy and faintly musky. Vaguely Oriental, it made pictures of lace and satin lingerie and silky skin flash through his mind. It went straight from his lungs into his bloodstream and he was probably going to need a cold shower to get rid of the physical reaction it generated.

His long legs stepped easily over the mounded snow, and J.D. balanced her on one knee while he pulled open the truck door and swung her onto the high seat.

"Thank you," Ashley sent him a grateful, slightly shaky smile and he nodded in brief acknowledgment before slamming the pickup door and rounding the front to climb behind the wheel.

He leaned back in the seat and shoved a hand into the pocket of his tight jeans to retrieve the keys. Faded denim strained across his lap and Ashley quickly averted her fascinated gaze. The truck's engine turned over with a muted roar. J.D.'s right hand moved over levers on the dash and a blast of cold air hit Ashley's legs.

"Oh! My goodness, that's cold!" she exclaimed.

"Sorry," chiselled lips lifted in an amused grin. Ashley stared helplessly. The smile crinkled his eyes and softened the hard lines of his face into heart-stopping handsomeness. "We'll have warm air in a few minutes." He leaned a forearm on the steering wheel and half-turned in the seat to look at her. "Where are you from? California? Florida, maybe? Didn't Joanne warn you that we have snow and freezing cold in Idaho in the winter?"

"I'm from New York—and yes, Joanne warned me." Ashley answered his smile with one of her own. "We have lots of snow and freezing cold in New York City, too, but I was working and didn't have time to change before I left for the airport this morning. As it was, I nearly missed my plane." She lifted one high-heeled foot and eyed it ruefully. "When my car died, I could see the lights of the bar and thought I wouldn't need to unlock my suitcases to get my boots. I can see now that I should have."

J.D. couldn't keep his gaze from sliding up the arch of her foot, across the slim curve of her ankle, and on up her calf until his hungry gaze was halted by the concealing fur.

He yanked his eyes away from her legs and shifted the truck into reverse. He twisted around, one arm propped on the back of the seat with one hand turning the wheel as he backed the truck out of the parking space.

"Which way is your car?"

His deep voice was abrupt, even brusque. Confused, Ashley shot him a searching glance. The smile was gone, the hard lines of his face once more seemed to be set in granite—remote and cool.

"That way—about three blocks, maybe three and a half." Ashley gestured to his left.

He didn't comment but silently revved the truck's powerful engine, his arm dropping from the seat back to shift into first gear, the hard muscles of his thigh bunching and flexing beneath worn denim as he worked the clutch.

Silence filled the cab, broken only by the engine's rumble and the crunch of snow beneath the tires. Ashley looked out the side window at the short few blocks of Main Street. The street itself was wide, far wider than the traffic-jammed streets of New York City. It was only ten-thirty at night, but except for streetlights the town was dark, the businesses closed and shuttered. Only a small cluster of vehicles, mostly four-wheel drive pickups with rifle racks in their back windows, slanted into parking places. The moon cast its silver light over the buildings, throwing black shadows across the mouths of alleys and out across sidewalks.

The truck's heater was finally blowing warm air and Ashley emitted an unconscious sigh, stretching out her toes to its beckoning heat.

"Take your shoes off. Your feet will get warm faster without the wet leather against them."

"Thanks—" Ashley slid her toes out of the pumps and rubbed one damp foot on top of the other. "There's my car," she suddenly sat upright and pointed out the windshield. "The little red compact."

J.D. swung the pickup around in a U-turn and pulled in behind the car. He half-turned to face her and held out his hand.

Her confused gaze went from his hand to his face.

"What?"

"The keys," he said patiently. "I need the keys to get your luggage."

"Oh, oh, of course!" She flushed and slid her hands into the coat's pockets. "Here they are."

She could have just dropped them into his open palm. She certainly meant to drop them. But when the keys touched his palm, his hand closed over both the metal and her fingers—and somehow, she couldn't let go. She stared up at him. Only a foot of upholstered leather seat separated them. The glow of the dash lights highlighted the thrust of high cheekbones, the dark shadows of his eyes beneath the brim of his hat, the full curve of his lower lip. The upper button of the denim jacket was unfastened and Ashley glimpsed the strong, tanned column of his throat inside the collar of a flannel blue plaid shirt. Her gaze shifted back to his eyes and she was trapped, enmeshed in the dark brown depths, unable to pull her gaze away from his.

J.D. was having trouble with his breathing. To tell the truth, it felt like the time a bronc kicked him in the chest. The touch of her small hand in his sent his heart shuddering into overdrive. The glow of the dash lights stroked her cheeks and lips with a golden brush and gleamed off that incredible mane of hair. He wanted to press his thumb against the velvety softness of her bottom lip and bury his face in her silky hair. He'd bet everything he owned that it smelled like she did too—sexy and sweet and all woman.

Her eyes glowed up at him, golden and soft with uncertain curiosity. Something twisted inside J.D., the hard, cold wall around his heart melted a little and a warm tide of protectiveness flooded him at the vulnerability he saw in the golden eyes and the sweet, soft curve of her mouth.

With an effort of iron will, he yanked his thoughts up short.

Oh no, McCullough! Not again! You were tangled up with one rich woman and once was enough! You're not doing it again—no matter how beautiful she is!

Gazing helplessly up into his hard face, Ashley saw his jaw harden and the sudden curtain that dropped to veil his dark eyes. A muscle flexed in his cheek and his fingers tugged the keys away from her.

"Sit tight," he said abruptly. "I'll be right back."

He tugged his hat lower over his brow and slid out of the truck, slamming the door behind him to trap the warmth inside the cab and seal away the frigid outside air.

Ashley inched her toes closer to the warm current blowing under the dashboard and watched J.D. as he unlocked the trunk and pulled out her belongings. The heavy suitcases and garment bag that she had struggled to load into the compact's small trunk looked weightless as he tucked one effortlessly under his arm and caught up the other two. The cab rocked gently when he tossed them in the truck bed. Ashley hunched her shoulders, her gaze following J.D.'s tall, broad body when he crossed in front of the truck's headlights to slam the compact's trunk lid.

She shifted on the seat and stared at the tall cowboy checking the locked doors of the car. *Why am I reacting to him like this?* She frowned, the action creasing a delicate vee between her sable brows. *I'm just tired*, she decided. *And it's probably a perfectly normal reaction to be fascinated with J.D. McCullough after listening to Joanne tell stories that made him seem larger-than-life. She had every girl in our college dormitory in love with him!*

J.D. walked around the front of the truck, boots crunching against the cold snow underfoot, and pulled open the door. A blast of cold air entered the cab with him, and Ashley shivered and pulled her coat closer.

He revved the powerful engine and shifted into first gear. The silver pickup nosed around the little red compact and gained speed as they left the town behind.

"Do you see Joanne and Blake often?" Ashley asked, her eyes on his profile which was etched by the dash light against the dark night outside the window.

"Yes, we're neighbors. I usually see them every day or so." A frown pulled down the dark brows and he added slowly, "Come to think of it, I haven't seen either of them for nearly a week. I've been busy and haven't stopped by their place and Blake hasn't come by the house."

"Do you suppose something is wrong?" Ashley asked. Her body inclined unconsciously toward his, her hair swinging against her cheek to frame her face with dark silk.

J.D. shot her a glance and immediately wished he hadn't. She was too damned sexy for her own good. Or his. One hand left the steering wheel to push a tape into the cassette player in the dashboard.

"No. I'm sure nothing's wrong." His words had that bitten-off tone again.

Ashley parted her lips to question him further, but a 1950's ballad poured out of the speakers making conversation impossible. She closed her mouth without asking him how he could be so sure.

She shifted back against the seat and gazed out of the truck's side window. The fields and pastures stretching beyond black fence posts were frozen white carpets dotted with the black shapes of pines. Like tall dark sentinels, the trees caught the moon's silver light and threw it back in inky shadows reaching from their trunks across the pristine white carpet of snow.

It's so beautiful. And so peaceful, she thought. The city seemed far away. She turned to share her sense of wonder with the man beside her, but J.D. was staring ahead, scowling at the windshield. She stifled the impulse and turned again to look out the window. She wondered if he were always this moody or if it was just that he was irritated that he had to deliver her to Joanne's. Ashley vaguely remembered Joanne mentioning that J.D. wasn't fond of women in general and she made a mental note to quiz her about the details.

J.D. turned the pickup off the highway into a long, snowy lane lined with barbed wire fences. The lane wound around the foot of a hill and then climbed the slope. Below them lay the buildings of a ranch. The long ranch house was dark and quiet.

"Are they expecting you?" J.D. asked, maneuvering the truck down the icy gravel lane.

"I'm sure they are. I wired Joanne two days ago saying that I'd be driving up from Boise today."

J.D. merely grunted in acknowledgment and swung the pickup to a halt in front of a yard gate that allowed entry to the snow-covered lawn. A shovelled sidewalk led to a wide porch and front door.

"Stay there," he ordered and pushed his door open. He rounded the hood of the truck and pulled open the passenger door. "There's a lot of snow out here." His deep voice was almost a growl. He slid his arms under and around her and lifted her out of the truck.

Ashley felt pampered and cherished, and realized with a shock that no one had ever made her feel that way before. She kept her gaze fastened on his jacket collar and refused to give in to the urge to search his face, but she couldn't ignore the feel of warm hands against her legs or the scent of male that assailed her nostrils. His boots rang in the silent night as he carried her across the broad porch. When he slid her gently to her feet she caught the front of his jacket to steady herself.

"Thank you," she murmured, slanting him a shy look from beneath her lashes.

"No problem," his deep voice was slightly husky and his hand left her back reluctantly. He stepped away from her and rang the doorbell.

A dog began to bark from somewhere inside the house. A porch light went on above their heads before the door swung inward, the glow of the hall lamp outlining Joanne's slim, five-foot-four frame. The lamp's soft light glinted off tousled reddish-blonde hair and the sleepy blue eyes were underscored with dark shadows against her fair, freckle-dusted skin. She clutched the lapels of a blue terrycloth robe together and blinked up at the broad-shouldered man at her door.

"J.D.? Is that you?" Surprise turned to worry. "What are you doing here in the middle of the night? Is something wrong?" Concern colored the lilting tones.

"It's not the middle of the night, Jo, it's barely eleven o'clock and no, there's nothing wrong." He shifted slightly to allow Joanne to look behind him. "I brought you an early Christmas present."

Amazed delight spread across Joanne's expressive features.

"Ashley!" She shoved the door open and caught Ashley in a hug that threatened to squeeze the life out of her. "Ashley! Why didn't you tell me you were coming? Oh, come in! Come in!" She caught J.D. and Ashley's arms and tugged them inside the entryway, releasing them just long enough to close the door behind them. "Come into the kitchen. Everybody's asleep."

Joanne hurried them down a dim hall, flipping on lights as she went. The house was blessedly warm; the kitchen a comfortable room with the lingering fragrance of baking. Cheery yellow-and-blue patterned wallpaper covered the walls from the ceiling down to wainscoting that was painted white. The maple dinette set's highbacked Shaker chairs boasted yellow-and-blue corduroy cushions. Bright copper-bottomed pans hung above an old-fashioned enamelled wood cookstove. Although the kitchen boasted a modern range, the cream-colored cookstove with its gleaming nickel trim held pride of place.

J.D. sniffed and a grin tilted his hard mouth.

"Chocolate chip?" He arched a black brow at Joanne as he lifted the top of a ceramic cookie jar shaped like a red apple.

"Of course." Joanne returned his smile before turning her back on him to give Ashley another hug. "I can't believe this! Why didn't you tell me you were coming?"

Ashley paused while sliding out of her coat.

"I did tell you. Didn't you get my telegram?"

"Heavens no! Did you send me one?"

"Yes, of course. I gave it to Magda to send—" Ashley's gaze met Joanne's and their gold and blue eyes both reflected instant understanding.

"Good old Aunt Maggie," Joanne said wryly. "She hasn't changed a bit, has she?"

"No, I'm afraid not." Ashley tossed her coat carelessly on a chair. "She threw a fit when I insisted on coming out here for Christmas."

"I suppose she had you booked through the holidays?"

"She tried," Ashley grimaced. "I told her six months ago not to book me through Christmas because I needed some time off. But you know Magda—she can't turn down a good offer.''

"Hah!" Joanne snorted inelegantly. "She can't turn down the opportunity to make more money from you, Ashley.'' She recognized the defensive protest in the gold gaze fixed on her and shook her head with regret. "I'm sorry, Ashley. You're in my house for five minutes and already I'm giving you a bad time about your aunt. I promise I'll hold my tongue and not do it again.''

"We both know *that* promise will last maybe ten minutes!" Ashley's laughter filled the kitchen with rich music and, after an impish look, Joanne joined her.

J.D. leaned against the butcher block countertop, long legs crossed at the ankle, jacket unbuttoned and arms folded across his chest while he munched on a chocolate chip cookie. *It's a good thing they've forgotten I'm here*, he reflected wryly. His curiosity about what lay beneath the fur coat was satisfied. And then some. Ever since Ashley shed the fur, he hadn't been able to take his eyes off her. She was wearing a long-sleeved white sweater dress with chunky gold jewelry, the necklace and earrings studded with topaz stones that matched her lioness eyes. The dress was soft angora and fell straight from the shoulders to just above her knees, with a cowl collar that draped softly around her slender neck. It was cinched in at the waist with a belt of the same material. She was fully covered

from neck to knees and shoulder to wrist, but the
demure cut was defeated by material that clung to
the thrust of full breasts and the indentation of her
tiny waist. J.D. was sure his two hands could span
her waist. His palms itched to touch her, to slide
from the crown of her silky head, down over the
soft angora to her feet, and back up again.

Staring at her was beginning to affect him physically and he forced his gaze away from Ashley to
Joanne's pale features. He'd been so absorbed in
his study of Ashley that he hadn't really looked at
the slender redhead before. But now that he did,
what he saw pulled his brows together in a frown.

"Joanne," he interrupted. The two women
stopped talking and turned to look at him. It was
clear that they had nearly forgotten his presence in
the happy excitement of being together again. "You
look like hell! And I haven't seen Blake in days."

"Thanks, J.D., you really know how to make a
girl feel good," Joanne wrinkled her nose at him
and smoothed a self-conscious hand over her tousled hair. "Blake's down with the flu and Cassie
has the mumps."

Ashley sat up straight in her chair and fixed a
concerned look on Joanne. She'd been so delighted
to see Joanne after so long that she hadn't noticed
how exhausted she appeared.

"Oh, Joanne, I shouldn't have come," her voice
was filled with contrition, as she noted her friend's
pale face and dark under-eye shadows. "The last
thing you need is a houseguest underfoot!"

"Nonsense, you're not a guest, you're family," Joanne said vehemently, shaking her head. "And as long as you've had the mumps and can put up with us—what is it?" She leaned across the table to search Ashley's worried features. "You have had the mumps, haven't you?"

"I don't think so, Joanne," Ashley answered slowly, her brow furrowing in thought. "At least, I don't remember having them."

"Oh, no!" Joanne groaned, her blue eyes widening with consternation. "Can you call your Aunt Maggie?"

"No—she's on a Caribbean cruise on a friend's yacht until after Christmas. They flew out for Jamaica an hour after my plane took off." Ashley tapped a manicured nail against her teeth in concentration and added almost to herself, "I could call Dr. Sanders in New York. He did all my annual checkups when I was a child. I'm sure he'd know if I ever had the mumps."

Joanne flicked a glance at the copper wall clock above the refrigerator.

"It must be after two A.M. in New York."

"You're right. I'd hate to disturb him at this hour—even if I knew his home number, which I don't."

"Oh, Ashley, this is terrible! You can't stay here until we find out if you're immune! For a child, mumps is just another unpleasant childhood disease. But for an adult, they're dangerous."

The two women stared at each other, disappointment stamped across their features.

"I'm sure I can reach him tomorrow," Ashley said slowly. "But what will we do about tonight?"

J.D. shifted where he leaned against the counter and Joanne's blue gaze flicked to his broad figure. Relief lit up her expressive, mobile face.

"You can stay at J.D.'s place!"

Joanne didn't seem to notice that her suggestion met with a complete lack of response on J.D.'s still, hard features and a quick flash of dismay on Ashley's before she quickly changed it to polite interest.

"It's the perfect solution. Your sister's old room is empty now that she's married, J.D., and you're practically right next door so she won't be far away," Joanne chattered happily on, oblivious to the silence from the other two occupants of the kitchen. "Don't you think it's the perfect solution, J.D.?"

J.D. eyed her bright face with a complete lack of expression.

Ashley felt an embarrassed flush warm her cheeks. Couldn't Joanne see that the man didn't want her company?

"I don't want to put Mr. McCullough to so much inconvenience, Joanne," she said quietly. "I'll take a room in town."

"You can't," Joanne answered. "There isn't a hotel in town."

"Oh," Once again, small teeth worried her lower lip. "Well then, perhaps I—"

"Joanne's right," J.D. interrupted her. "You'll stay at my place. It's the only solution that makes sense. I've got an empty bedroom—more than one actually."

"That's very kind of you, Mr. McCullough, but I don't think—"

J.D. cut off her protest with a decisive movement of one big hand.

"Just neighborly, Miss Tierney. Now, if you two don't mind, I've got a long day tomorrow and you both look like you're ready to drop. I suggest we all get to bed."

He pushed away from the counter and looked at her, hands on hips, impatient to be gone.

Ashley's gaze went from Joanne's beaming face to J.D.'s unreadable, handsome countenance. For some reason, she was hesitant—no, almost afraid—to go with the tough cowboy. Something happened to her every time he pinned her with those dark eyes, and just being in the same room with him set the hair at her nape prickling with awareness.

But she was too tired to puzzle it all out now. The long hours spent holding poses in the cold dawn, followed by the long flight and the drive to Antelope had exhausted her. It was just possible that after a good night's sleep, all of this would fall into perspective and J.D. McCullough would be just another man. She hoped.

She pinned a smile on her face and answered him calmly.

"Very well, but I still hate to impose on your kindness. I'm sure I'll be able to reach Dr. Sanders tomorrow."

"Right." J.D. tugged his hat lower and crossed the room in two long strides to pick up Ashley's coat from its resting place against the bright yellow corduroy cushion on the maple dinette chair. "Let's get going. You look like you're out on your feet and so does Joanne."

Ashley gave him a glance from between thick lashes that told him what she thought of his high-handedness, but he met it with a noncommital expression and held the coat for her. She rose and slid her arms into the sleeves. J.D.'s fingers didn't linger on her shoulders, and she pushed down a surge of regret at the briefness of their touch and turned to face Joanne.

"I'll call you as soon as I talk to the doctor tomorrow."

Joanne threw her arms around Ashley and hugged her fiercely.

"You do that—the very *minute* you get off the line."

Ashley's grip was just as fierce. She had come so far and to have to leave Joanne when she had barely arrived brought her to the edge of tears. The two women left the kitchen and walked down the hallway to the front door.

"J.D. will take good care of you, Ashley,"

Joanne whispered softly. "He's closer to me than my own brother."

Ashley smiled and nodded without comment.

J.D. held the door open and waited while Ashley and Joanne exchanged a last hug. When Ashley stepped over the threshold onto the front porch, he bent and swung her up into his arms, ignoring Joanne's astounded expression.

"See you tomorrow, Joanne. Tell Blake I'll be by to see him and run a check on the cattle for him."

Ashley linked her arms around his neck with the ease of familiarity and called good-bye over her shoulder. Fortunately for her peace of mind, she couldn't see the look of stunned shock on her best friend's face or hear her muttered words of delighted disbelief. Joanne was an incorrigible matchmaker and one look at her face would have warned Ashley that trouble was in the wind.

This time the truck wasn't as cold, but Ashley was still relieved when the heater started blowing warm air against her feet and ankles. She slanted a sideways glance at J.D.'s broad bulk, her eyes drawn to his hand on the gearshift. A light dusting of black hair against tanned skin covered his wrists where the denim jacket sleeves slid up as he shifted the gears. His hands were wide, the fingers square-tipped, fingernails pared and clean. She grew warm remembering the touch of those hands, rough with callouses, against the sensitive backs of her knees.

Odd, she frowned, confused. *I never thought knees were supposed to be erogenous zones.* She forced her gaze away from his hand and the memories it evoked.

"Is it far to your ranch, J.D.?"

He liked the way she said his name. Husky and sexy as hell.

"No—maybe ten minutes." He glanced sideways at her. She was snuggled down into the soft fur of her coat. The dash light etched the classic line of small nose and the droop of soft mouth. The thick lashes seemed to weigh down her eyelids; they drooped sleepily over gold irises. "Close your eyes if you want, I'll wake you when we get there."

Ashley couldn't summon the energy to respond. Instead, she meekly did as he directed and allowed her eyes to close.

It seemed only moments before a cold blast of air touched her face and she shivered, mumbling and pulling away from the hand that shook her.

"Ashley, wake up. Ashley—Ashley! Ashley! Oh, hell."

Strong arms slid under her and she snuggled close to the warm, hard body, nuzzling her face against the warmth of soft, male-scented skin.

"Mmmmmhh, you smell good," she mumbled drowsily, normal inhibitions erased by near-sleep.

"Oh yeah?" The deep male voice was laced with amusement. "I probably smell like horses, smoke, and beer."

"Nope," she pushed her nose against the warm skin of his neck beneath his ear. "Man. You smell like man. I like it."

The arms around her tightened, muscles flexing in instant response to her unconsciously provocative statement.

"I'm glad." This time the voice was definitely husky, all amusement vanished.

"Are we home yet?" she asked fuzzily, unwilling to leave the dreamlike state between sleep and consciousness.

"Yeah, honey," the deep voice was gravelly. It seemed somehow right for the arms that held her to hug her possessively closer. "We're home."

"Oh good," she yawned daintily and stopped struggling to get her eyes open. "Then I can go to sleep. I'm so tired."

J.D. carried his precious burden across his porch and into the silent house. He didn't want to wake Ashley, so he didn't turn on the lights. He didn't need them anyway. He could have found his way around the big, two-story house blindfolded. He'd been born in the master bedroom's big oak bedstead that he now called his own and, except for the two years he had spent in the army and the six months in the hospital after Saigon, he'd spent all of his thirty-three years on the McCullough spread.

He climbed the stairway, automatically avoiding the squeaky third step, and carried Ashley into his sister's old room. He bent to set her on the cream-

and-pink bedspread, but her arms wouldn't release him and he pried them loose with gentle hands.

She didn't waken and he indulged himself for long moments, allowing his eyes the luxury of staring at her. The moonlight that fingered its way past sheer white curtains and into the room gleamed off the mane of dark brown hair fanned across the pillow. Her thick lashes made dark crescents against soft cheeks; the soft, lush mouth relaxed and vulnerable in sleep.

J.D. felt an unfamiliar urge to protect her. While he was still struggling to understand the alien emotion, Ashley sighed and shifted against the pink-and-creme bedspread.

J.D.'s gaze slid lower and he frowned. She was still wrapped in the heavy fur coat, the wet black shoes still covering silk-clad feet. He couldn't leave her to sleep all night dressed as she was. She'd be uncomfortable as hell.

He dropped his hat on the chair by the window and shrugged out of his coat before checking the thermostat. The dial registered only sixty-six degrees. He'd have to blame his rising body temperature on something else.

He turned back to the bed where Ashley slept peacefully, blissfully unaware of his rising temperature. It took several moments to pull her out of the coat. She was completely uncooperative, her soft body boneless. The shoes were easier; he slid them off her feet easily, telling himself that he was only testing the elegant bones of her toes and ankles for warmth when his hands insisted on lingering over the silk-clad skin.

He backed away from the bed and the woman on it, and quietly opened the closet to take out a down comforter. As he approached the bed Ashley shifted, rolling onto her side and curling her hands beneath her cheek. The movement slid the soft angora dress higher until the hem rode halfway up her thigh, exposing the top of dark stockings with lacy, cream garters and a strip of smooth skin, which was tan against the white angora.

J.D.'s throat went dry and his palms itched. He swallowed several times and yanked his eyes away from her legs. A quick glance at her face assured him that those gold eyes were still closed. His black gaze returned to the length of enticing leg, and that two inches of bare, soft skin.

His fists clenched until the knuckles turned white. A muscle jumped in his jaw and he found it impossible to stop looking at her. It had been a long time since he'd had a woman. Too long. And he'd never had one that came close to his fantasies. She wasn't wearing the conventional panty hose that most women wore—she was wearing that garter belt with lacy, cream garters. J.D. closed his eyes against the images that popped into his head about what else she may—or may not—be wearing under the soft angora dress.

He didn't know how long he stood there—just

stood there—staring at her, but Ashley shifted again, murmuring in her sleep, and the movement and sound snapped him out of his trance. Her leg moved higher and the garters pulled tighter, pressing into her soft skin and making a red mark against the unblemished smoothness.

J.D. frowned. It didn't look comfortable and it was clearly irritating the smooth skin of her leg, but he was damned if he was going to touch her to take the things off. She could just sleep in them. He refused to admit, even to himself, that he wasn't sure what he might do if he touched the satiny smooth skin that lured him until a sweat broke out on his brow. With quick decisiveness, he shook out the comforter over the bed and watched it settle softly over the sleeping woman, concealing the temptation of Ashley's curving long legs, soft breasts, and narrow waist above flaring hips.

Ashley sighed and snuggled contentedly beneath the soft warmth of the comforter, never knowing that the hard-faced outlaw who treated her with such gentleness watched her for another moment before yanking his hat and coat off the chair and turning on his heel to abruptly leave the room.

THREE

Warm light tapped gently, but insistently, on Ashley's closed eyelids. Reluctantly, she half opened them and turned her face away from the sunlight that beamed through sheer-white curtains. Frowning, she let her gaze roam over the unfamiliar bedroom. She was lying on a walnut four-poster bed in a large, square bedroom that was decidedly old-fashioned. There was no question that it was a woman's room. A tall armoire that matched the bed's gleaming walnut stood next to a closet door on the far wall and matching nightstands flanked the comfortable bed.

Remembrance came swiftly. This was J.D. McCullough's house, not Joanne's. And unlike

Joanne, her host was *not* delighted to have her as a guest.

She pushed back the soft comforter and sat up before realizing that she was still wearing the dress she had traveled in yesterday. Her fur coat lay across a chair near the door, her suitcases stacked beside it. Her black pumps rested neatly under the chair on the plush, blue carpet.

She swung her legs over the edge of the bed, silk-covered toes curling reflexively to test the soft thickness of the carpet while she took off her earrings and necklace and dropped them on the nightstand. The angora dress was wrinkled and she pushed the tangle of dark hair away from her face before standing to untie the sash and pull the softly clinging garment off. She dropped it on the bed and then unhooked the garters to peel off the dark silk hosiery. It only took a few moments to rummage through one of her suitcases, find a jade-silk kimono, and wrap herself in it. Catching up the clear vinyl bag holding toiletries and makeup, Ashley opened the bedroom door and peeked out into the hall.

The hall was empty; the whole house was silent. Ashley moved cautiously down the hallway until she found the white-and-yellow tile bathroom. It smelled of soap and men's cologne; a still-damp towel hung over the bar next to the shower door. The undeniable presence of a man permeated the room and Ashley breathed deeply, savoring the scent of aftershave and the sight of a razor resting neatly next to an aerosol can of shaving cream. The unfamiliarity of sharing a bathroom with a man was intriguing.

Her Aunt Magda had a never-ending parade of male friends, but none of them had ever taken up residence in the Park Avenue apartment paid for with income from Ashley's modeling. Ashley herself neither had the time nor the inclination to pursue a steady relationship and, as a consequence, had never awakened in a man's house. So the male articles left by J.D. were new and fascinating in their novelty. But Ashley refused to consider that the fascination was generated more by J.D. than men in general.

By the time Ashley had showered, applied a light covering of makeup, pulled the sable hair into a ponytail, and dressed in narrow-legged jeans and turquoise sweater, it was nearly noon. She felt blissfully decadent. She couldn't remember the last time she had a vacation and been allowed to sleep past five A.M.

It took only a few moments to plump the pillows and straighten the bedding. She folded and spread the soft down-filled comforter across the foot of the bed. Venturing into the hall again, she paused and listened intently before opening the other two doors in the hall. Both were bedrooms. One was clearly a guest room done in cool greens with a walnut bed and matching dresser. The other room was unmistakably, definitely J.D.'s domain. Curious, Ashley ventured inside. The old oak bedstead looked as if it had crossed the plains in a covered wagon and on closer inspection Ashley suspected it had. The rest of the bedroom furniture— a tall, oak dresser and 1800's washstand that served as a bedside table, a large carved-oak grandfather rocker—was as old, as sturdy, and as proportionately big as the bed. A red plaid workshirt was slung over the arm of the rocker and the closet doors stood ajar to reveal shirts, jeans, slacks, and sweaters on hangers above a row of boots and shoes. The room smelled faintly of the cologne scent in the bathroom, a scent Ashley remembered clinging to J.D.'s skin when he caught her up and carried her above the snow.

Ashley stopped herself abruptly, snatching her fingers from the oak bedpost where they unconsciously stroked the worn, satiny smooth wood.

Why am I standing here daydreaming over J.D. McCullough?

She turned on her heel and left the room, her stride determined and purposeful as she moved down the hallway and stairs.

The quiet that ruled upstairs also held sway on the lower floor. Ashley poked her head into a living room and office before locating the kitchen. The house was old-fashioned and charming but the no-frills sparseness clearly indicated its resident was a man. No pillows were plumped against the early American sofa facing a huge, rough stone fireplace, and the large leather recliner was built to accomodate a man's frame. No green plants or flowers added their fragrance to the rooms, and the dominant colors were earth tones.

The kitchen was a square, wide room with plenty of space for a table and four chairs in the windowed alcove. Pale winter sunlight poured through the windows and lit the room with a welcome, sunny cheer. Ashley crossed the green-and-white linoleum floor to the knotty-pine cabinets and a phone attached to the wall next to the back door that led out onto an enclosed porch.

A dial tone hummed in her ear and Ashley quickly punched in the telephone information sequence for New York City and got Dr. Sanders's office number.

"Good afternoon," a pleasant voice came on the line. "Dr. Sanders's answering service. May I help you?"

"I need to speak with Dr. Sanders, please. It's important."

"I'm sorry. Dr. Sanders is out of town for the Christmas holidays—in the Bahamas, I believe. But Dr. Oakland is taking all of his emergency calls. I'll connect you with his nurse—"

"No, wait," Ashley interrupted before her call could be transferred. "I don't need an appointment to see the doctor." Quickly, she explained her problem, but although the woman was sympathetic, she couldn't help.

"All of your records would be stored at Dr. Sanders's office and Dr. Oakland wouldn't have access to them. I'm afraid it will be impossible to locate the information you need until Dr. Sanders returns, which won't be for another two weeks. I can try to locate his nurse, if you like, but I don't know if I'll be successful."

Reluctantly, Ashley had to be satisfied with her offer and with a promise that she would call back the moment she had any information about the nurse. She thanked her and hung up, staring unseeingly out the window at the snow-covered landscape.

Should she gamble that she was safe and wouldn't catch the mumps or should she return to New York? She hated to give up and leave Idaho. Her schedule was so hectic that heaven alone knew when she could manage to free up another two weeks.

With a troubled sigh, she rang information for Joanne's telephone number and dialed it.

"Ashley!" Joanne's voice bubbled over the line. "I was beginning to wonder if you were going to call! Did you just wake up?"

"Yes," Ashley smiled, twisting the telephone cord around her index finger. "I can hardly believe I slept until nearly noon. I haven't done that in years!"

"That's because you haven't had a real vacation in years," Joanne retorted. "Did you reach Dr. Sanders?"

"Sort of."

"What do you mean sort of?"

Ashley quickly explained the problem.

"I don't know what to do," she concluded. "I hate to turn around and fly back to New York, but on the other hand, I hate to take a chance and catch Cassie's mumps."

"Don't do either," Joanne said firmly. "Stay right where you are until the answering service finds Dr. Sanders's nurse."

"Stay here? In J.D.'s house?" Ashley squeaked in surprised shock. "Are you crazy? I can't possibly do that!"

"Why not?" Joanne demanded.

"I hardly know the man! And he hardly knows me! What makes you think he'd let me stay in his house indefinitely?"

"Oh, for heavens sakes, Ashley! You're overreacting. Besides, it will probably only be for a few days—just until the service can locate Dr. Sanders's nurse." She was met with silence from Ashley. "Please," she cajoled. "I haven't seen you for over two years. I can't bear for you to turn around and go back East. At least if you're at J.D.'s house, I can talk to you by phone everyday. And," she added, "if you go back to New York now your aunt will have you booked solid and working every day, and you won't have a moment's rest.''

In spite of Ashley's misgivings about how J.D. McCullough was going to feel about having her as an unwanted guest, she knew exactly how Joanne felt about cutting short this visit because she felt the same way. Joanne was her closest friend. For Ashley, orphaned at eight and raised by a series of housekeepers, Joanne became the sister she had always wanted when they were assigned to share a dorm room at an upstate New York college. For four years the two had been inseparable. Then came graduation. Ashley reluctantly returned to New York City to resume full-time modeling under her aunt's demanding tutelage, while Joanne returned to Idaho to marry her rancher fiancé. In the three years since graduation, Joanne flew to New York City once to visit, and Ashley had been in Seattle and San Francisco on two separate assignments when Blake and Joanne decided to visit her in those cities. The last visit in San Francisco had been over two years ago.

"I don't want to leave Idaho any more than you want me to go back to the East Coast, Joanne," Ashley conceded, torn between her desire to stay and her reluctance to ask J.D. McCullough to extend his hospitality. "But I simply do not know Mr. McCullough well enough to ask him to let me live under his roof for any longer!"

"With any luck, it won't be for more than a few

days," Joanne said reassuringly. "The answering service might locate the doctor's nurse by tomorrow."

"Or they might not find her at all," Ashley said gloomily.

"Don't be such a pessimist," Joanne chided. "They'll probably locate her any day. She'll check the records, we'll find out you're perfectly safe if you're exposed to Cassie's germs, you'll move into my guest room, and we'll have a wonderful Christmas!"

Ashley laughed and gave in.

"All right, all right! I give up. I'll talk to J.D. when he comes in and explain the situation. But I warn you, Joanne, if I think he really doesn't want me here, I'm catching the next plane back to New York."

"He won't mind, I promise!" Joanne said happily. She glanced out her kitchen window and saw J.D.'s tall, broad-shouldered body crossing the lot between the barn and the house. *Especially after I talk to him!* "Oh goodness, Ashley, I hear Cassie crying!" she said with a fine disregard for the truth. "I have to run! I'll call you later."

Joanne hung up the phone and opened the kitchen door to call out to J.D. While his long strides ate up the distance between them, her brain was racing. In that brief moment the night before when J.D. stood on her front porch with Ashley cradled in his arms, she saw a gentleness in him she thought was lost more than ten years before. And

Ashley's usual distant politeness toward men had been replaced by a shyly trusting curiosity. Joanne couldn't help rejoicing over the unexpected opportunity to make a match between her two favorite people.

Ashley wasn't looking forward to asking the rough rancher if she could use his sister's bedroom for another night or two. In spite of Joanne's reassurances, she couldn't forget J.D.'s face when Joanne suggested she stay in his sister's vacant bedroom. Granted, he hadn't said he didn't want her in his house, but then he hadn't said he wanted her there, either. In fact, his total lack of expression left her assuming that he wasn't pleased by the turn of events.

She sighed and decided that worrying wasn't going to help. She glanced around the bright kitchen. It had a good, solid feeling about it, as if it had been planned with a family in mind, although Ashley knew from Joanne that J.D. was a bachelor. The knotty-pine cabinets and white stove and refrigerator spoke of a 1950's remodeling and Ashley assumed that J.D.'s mother had been responsible for the homey kitchen. A solitary coffee mug was rinsed and left to dry in the white-porcelain sink. A coffeepot rested on the white-enameled stove. She crossed to the stove and touched the pot with tentative fingers. It was stone cold. J.D. must have been gone for hours. She wondered briefly if he would be coming home for lunch, but a quick glance at the wall clock above the white refrigerator told her that it was nearly one o'clock and far past lunchtime.

That's encouraging, she thought with relief. *If he doesn't come home until dinnertime, I'll have that much longer before I have to ask him if I can continue on as his uninvited guest.*

Making dinner would be a good idea, she decided. Since cooking was one of her passions— one in which she rarely indulged due to the strict diet required by her career—cooking dinner would keep her from fretting the afternoon away. Briskly, she pushed up her sleeves and opened the freezer to check the contents.

At six P.M., J.D. pushed open the door leading from the back porch into the kitchen and halted abruptly on the threshold. There hadn't been a woman in his kitchen since his sister married and left home five years before. The sight was a distinct shock.

Ashley stood with her back to him, pot lid in one hand and spoon in the other, stirring something that steamed gently in a saucepan on the stove. A white dish towel was tied around her waist, the knot emphasizing her narrow waist above the curve of her hips and slender thighs encased in snug, worn blue jeans. Her hair was caught up into a ponytail, the nape of her neck innocently vulnerable beneath the youthful fall of silky hair.

The radio was tuned to a soft-rock station and she sang softly—brief, melodic snatches of the tune interspersed with contented humming as her body moved from side-to-side with the beat.

The warm, well-lit kitchen was filled with the aroma of baking. J.D.'s stunned glance found two pies cooling on the countertop, the lattice-tops oozing with cinnamon and apple juice. The aroma tugged enticingly at his nostrils, the same way the unexpectedly homey scene tugged at his heart-strings. He was hit with a sudden nostalgic flash from his boyhood; of racing into the kitchen on a winter night to find the warmth and comfort of his mother making dinner. He could almost see his father catching her around the waist and tickling her with cold fingers while she giggled and threatened him with a sticky spoon.

But they were only memories. His parents had been gone for nearly five years now, victims of a small plane crash near Boise. And gone long before the accident was the naive certainty of his boyhood dreams that he, too, would know an enduring love like the one his parents shared.

He remembered his earlier conversation with Joanne, and his deep seated suspicion of women and their motives kicked into gear. A familiar bitter, empty feeling settled in his gut.

Ashley replaced the lid on the saucepan and

turned to rinse the spoon at the sink. She froze in midstride at the sight of J.D. The black eyes held a fierce bitterness that paralyzed her vocal chords.

When he continued to look at her without comment, she stumbled nervously into speech.

"I made dinner," she said inanely, waving the sticky spoon toward the alcove table set with a linen cloth and dinnerware. "I hope you don't mind."

The black gaze left hers and flickered over the white tablecloth, china, napkins, and silverware.

"I found the cloth and the china in the bureau in the dining room."

His hard gaze moved back to Ashley.

"Nice," he drawled, folding his arms across his chest and leaning one broad flannel-covered shoulder against the door frame. "Now, I wonder why you went to so much trouble?"

Ashley frowned at him, confused by the hard, almost cynical smile on his scarred face. The black eyes fixed on her were coolly inscrutable.

"It wasn't any trouble," she answered slowly. "I like to cook. It's one of my favorite hobbies and I had nothing else to do this afternoon. I thought it was the least I could do to repay you for your hospitality."

"Is that the only reason?" he asked with deceptive mildness, one black brow arching in inquiry.

"What other reason could I have had?" she asked, puzzled.

"I thought maybe this was part of the softening-up process. Isn't there an old saying, 'The way to a man's heart is through his stomach.' "

Confused surprise quickly gave way to rising anger. Ashley glared at him, thick lashes narrowing over gold eyes. She could feel her cheeks flush with heat while she struggled to remain calm.

"In this instance, Mr. McCullough, I'm afraid the saying doesn't apply," she said with frigid politeness.

"Really?" He eyed her with a cynicism she was quickly beginning to dislike intensely. "You don't need to play this game, honey. Joanne already asked me if you could stay here on the Lazy M for a few days and I told her yes. So all this," he waved a hand toward the stove and table, "isn't necessary. You can go back to doing your nails, or whatever you occupy your time with in New York City during the afternoons, and I'll go back to cooking my own dinner."

Ashley listened to his speech with openmouthed amazement. When he finished, she stared at him— astounded—for a moment before her mouth snapped shut in a straight, tight line. She planted her fists on her hips, the golden eyes sizzling with outrage.

"Now, you listen to me, Mr. Hotshot Macho Cowboy! I do *not* spend my afternoons filing my nails. And I did *not* cook dinner to impress you. I cooked dinner because I love to cook and because *normal* people like to eat a hot meal after working all day." She paused to draw breath; she was so angry she expected to feel steam emitting from her ears. "Furthermore, I wouldn't stay under your roof for another minute, let alone a few days!"

J.D. stared at her with reluctant fascination. She was furious. Her skin fairly glowed with her rage, the golden eyes snapping with anger, the small fists belligerently propped on her hips, clenched until the knuckles were white. She wasn't the slightest bit intimidated by him. It was apparent that it hadn't even occurred to her to be afraid of him. It was such a novelty to have a woman stand up to him that a reluctant smile tugged at the corners of his hard mouth.

Ashley spied the upward quirk of his lips and her anger burned higher.

"Don't you dare laugh at me!" she ordered furiously.

"Yes, ma'am," he said meekly, black eyes losing their hard stare and actually twinkling with amusement.

Ashley glared at him for another moment. Infuriating man! First he accused her of trying to—to—to what? Seduce him. Or entrap him. Or entice him. Or whatever other crimes that arrogant male mind of his had conjured up. And now he just stood there—all tall, dark, and disgustingly handsome six feet of him—and smiled at her as if he found her cute.

She tossed the spoon in the sink with a clatter

and tugged impatiently at the knotted towel around her waist until it came free. She crumpled it into a ball and threw it on the counter, narrowly missing the pies. When she turned and marched toward the door that led to the dining room, J.D. pushed away from the door frame and stepped quickly in front of her. Ashley stepped to one side but he matched her movement. She tried again, but he reached out and caught her upper arms. His hands closed gently, but firmly, over her biceps. She knew better than to test the latent power in those muscle-corded arms by trying to pull free, so she halted and stared defiantly up into his hard face.

"Well?" she demanded, refusing to back down or to give an inch.

"I'm sorry," he began.

"Humph!" she interrupted with disdain, somehow managing to look down her nose at him even though he towered over her by half a foot.

"I said I'm sorry," he went on. "I'll admit I jumped to conclusions when I walked in and found you playing Suzy Homemaker after Joanne already told me she wanted you to stay here."

Ashley stiffened under his hand, gold eyes darkening stormily.

"I was *not* playing Suzy Homemaker. I like to cook."

"Okay, okay!" J.D. winced. "So you like to cook! You have to admit that baking pies doesn't exactly fit your image." Black eyes scanned the soft, flushed cheeks, the hot golden eyes, and the full curve of her bare lips. She didn't like that comment either, he realized. Those thick, inch-long eyelashes were narrowing over her eyes again. "Now what did I say wrong?"

"What did you mean by that crack about my image?" she demanded hotly.

"Only that you live a pretty glamorous life," he pointed out with perfect rationale. "I'm sure you're more at home in a slinky dress at a cocktail party than wearing jeans standing over a hot stove."

Ashley stiffened under his hold and fixed him with a hot, golden stare while she struggled to rein in her temper. In some part of her mind, she was astonished to find that she was so angry. No man had ever before stirred her enough to make her anything other than mildly repulsed. None of her reactions to J.D. McCullough was proving to be even remotely akin to any prior emotions aroused by any male.

"I am sick of people assuming that I'm an air-headed party girl just because I model clothes for a living!" she snarled through clenched teeth. "For your information, I graduated *cum laude* from college and I work hard. I rarely attend parties of any kind unless they're business related because I have to be in bed by nine o'clock every night. And I hate to further ruin my image, but I not only cook, I also do needlepoint. I'm not pro-miscuous, I don't do drugs, and I want to get married and have two point five kids and a dog someday—just like a lot of other women in America.''

J.D.'s amazed, incredulous expression would have been comical if Ashley hadn't been too furious to appreciate the humor.

She lifted one small hand and unclenched a fist to stab a forefinger at the hard chest beneath the blue-plaid shirt.

"Furthermore, you're perfectly safe. Don't worry about me trying to reach your heart through your stomach!''

"Really?'' he asked. "Why?''

Taken aback by his mellow response to her tirade, she stared at him for a moment before gathering her wits to answer.

"Never mind,'' she said truculently, "just take my word for it.

"But why?'' he insisted. "Is it because of this?''

He slid a finger down his cheek.

"What?'' she asked, startled. Her gaze flickered over his dark face and the thin, pale line that ran down his cheek. "Heavens no! It has nothing to do with *you*.''

J.D. gave his head a shake, as if to rearrange disconnected thoughts.

"Hold it. I think I missed something somewhere,'' he said slowly, releasing her. "You said I'm safe, that you won't try to worm your way into my affections through my stomach. But then you say it has nothing to do with me.'' He looked at her in total confusion, a slightly bewildered frown pulling black brows down over the night-dark eyes.

"It doesn't," Ashley said firmly, wishing fervently that her tongue hadn't run away with her. At his continued look of confusion, she raked her hair back off her temple with agitation. "Look, it has nothing to do with you, that's all." He continued to stare at her, clearly neither understanding nor accepting her response. "It's just me, that's all. I don't try to entice men."

His black eyes registered surprised disbelief coupled with wry amusement.

"Honey, with your looks, you don't need to *try*. It just happens."

"Oh, that," Ashley waved a dismissing hand. "That's just the image. It has nothing to do with me."

"You could have fooled me," he drawled. "I would have sworn that face and body were all yours!"

"Of course they are," she said impatiently. "But what men think of me—what they think I'm really like—is just a reflection of an ad campaign. I'm really not a sexy, seductive woman. It's all pretend."

J.D. stared at her as if she had lost her mind, so she continued impatiently.

"I'm not a very—you know—a very physical woman."

"Not physical?" He thought over her comment before comprehension dawned in his black eyes. "Are you trying to tell me in a roundabout way that you're frigid?" he asked bluntly.

"I *hate* that word!"

His black gaze roamed over her face, which was flushed with hectic color. It lingered over the proud tilt of her small chin, the soft mouth with its perfectly bowed upper lip, and the lower lips lush fullness before drifting lower—all the way to her toes—and then returning to meet her defiant gold stare.

"Who told you that?" he asked softly, disbelievingly.

"That's not important," she replied with embarrassed evasiveness.

"I can guess," he said shrewdly. "You told some man you wouldn't go to bed with him, and to save his ego he told you you were cold. Isn't that how it went?"

"No," she responded hastily. J.D.'s black eyes chided her and her cheeks burned warmer. "Well, not exactly," she amended. "Sort of, but not exactly."

"Just how close is not exactly?" he prodded.

"You don't give up, do you?" she asked in exasperation. "Oh, all right! It wasn't just one man, it was every man I ever dated. They all seemed to think that because of my work I was some sort of sex-hungry playgirl. I could put up with them wanting to kiss me good night, but when they started groaning and grabbing parts of my body, I just froze.''

"They?" he asked curiously. "Did this happen more than once?"

"Yes," she sighed and admitted after a pause, "with everyone I ever dated. I've been modeling since I was a child—that stupid image has been with me forever. Finally, I just stopped dating, except for agency-arranged business functions."

He shook his head in disbelief.

"You don't date?" His black stare focused intently on her mouth. "Honey, there's no way any woman with a mouth like yours and that much temper is frigid." His gaze met hers, the deep voice laden with calm conviction. "You've been seeing the wrong men."

A current of sexual tension stretched tautly between them and Ashley realized with a start that only a few inches separated her from his broad body. He gave off a heat that warmed her and the pleasing smell of shaving soap and man teased her nostrils. She took a hasty step backward.

"But you don't believe it, right?" he asked shrewdly, not missing her hasty retreat.

"I'm afraid not," she replied. "If you'll let me pass, I'll go get my bags."

"Wait a minute," his hand closed over her arm to detain her, the calloused fingers generating a warmth that tingled through her body and settled in her abdomen. "Forget about packing your bags. I'm sorry if I jumped to the wrong conclusion about dinner. I have a little trouble trusting women."

Big, golden eyes stared with solemn uncertainty up into his hard face, weighing whether or not she should believe him.

"If you don't stay," he added cajolingly, "Joanne will never forgive me."

A reluctant smile tugged at the soft corners of her mouth.

"Nor me," she acknowledged. "Are you sure I won't be in the way? I won't be any trouble?"

J.D. stared down at her, his hard face impassive.

Trouble? Was she kidding? If you discounted that fact that he'd spend the next few days taking cold showers and breaking into a sweat to keep from "grabbing parts of her body," hell no, she wouldn't be any trouble!

He took one final look at her serious, worried face and gave in with a silent sigh.

What the hell! It was only for a few days. Even if experience told him she was simply too good to be true.

"You won't be in the way and you won't be any trouble," he lied with a perfectly straight face. He drew in a deep breath, nostrils flaring. A wide smile curled his mouth and once more carved those fascinating dents in his cheeks. "And if that food tastes even half as good as it smells, I just might refuse to let you leave."

Ashley scanned his face intently before deciding he was sincere. A smile of relief lit her face.

"It's ready whenever you are."

"Give me fifteen minutes to shower and shave and I'll be right down."

He strode out of the room. Ashley stood still for a moment, listening to him take the stairs two at a time and rubbing her arm as if she could relieve the tingle that remained.

An hour later, J.D. leaned back in his chair and groaned with pleasure.

"Woman, you were right. You definitely *can* cook."

Ashley glowed with pleasure at the sincerity of the compliment.

"I'm going to tell all the women in town that the way to your heart really *is* through your stomach," she said teasingly, smiling at him over the rim of her coffee cup.

J.D.'s lashes narrowed threateningly over his black eyes. She smiled innocently and he gave a mental shrug, deciding she was teasing.

"You do and I'll tell all the men in New York that you're a fraud and you're really Betty Crocker in disguise. You'll be beating them off with sticks to keep them out of your kitchen instead of your bedroom."

"Okay," she laughed. "You win."

J.D. watched her while she sipped her coffee. She looked like a carefree, mischievous ten-year-old with that thick mane of silk pulled back in a ponytail and that lush mouth bare of lipstick. Her ponytail swung forward as she bent slightly to return the cup to its saucer. A smudge of whipped cream from her pie was nestled at the corner of her mouth. Without thinking, J.D. stretched out a hand to cup her chin and wipe it off.

Ashley turned her startled eyes to his.

"You had whipped cream on your face," he said with an indulgent smile, his thumb unconsciously continuing to stroke the delicate line of her jaw and the soft skin next to her lips.

"Oh," she whispered, unable to pull away from his warm stare and the mesmerizing stroke of his fingers. Like a kitten, she wanted to purr and stretch and rub her face against his fingers and palm. Confused and uneasy with the unaccustomed pleasure she found in a man's touch, she blinked and removed her chin from his grasp.

"Yes, well," she averted her gaze and quickly pushed back her chair to stand. "I'll just clear away the dishes."

"I'll help," he started to stand and reached to pick up the platter of roast beef and honey-glazed carrots, but Ashley stopped him.

"No, no really. I can manage."

"All right." Seeing that she was insistent, J.D. gave in, suddenly uncomfortable with the intimacy between them. "I have book work to do that I can't put off for another night. There's a tv and

VCR in the den, and a collection of movies in the cabinet. Or there are bookshelves in the den if you feel like reading.''

"Thank you. I think I'll find a book and make an early night of it,'' Ashley flashed him a smile, grateful that she would have a respite from the dizzyingly swift surges of emotion she felt, and the sexual tension that seemed to lie in wait ready to spring forth between them.

"Fine,'' he said brusquely. He hesitated as if to say more, but instead gave her an abrupt good night and left the room.

FOUR

By ten o'clock the next morning, Ashley had eaten breakfast, straightened the kitchen, dusted and vacuumed the living room, checked with the answering service in New York—only to be told that the nurse hadn't been found—and spent forty-five minutes on the phone chatting with Joanne.

She picked up the Dean Koontz thriller she had started the previous night and ruffled quickly through the pages before dropping it back onto the oak end table by the sofa. Too restless to read, she pulled back the drapes in the living room to gaze out across the snow-covered lawn.

The snow lay in a pristine white carpet and frosted the evergreen trees around the house. It lay in small white piles on the bare branches of a gnarled old apple tree, and highlighted, as if with an artist's brush, the beautifully symmetrical branches of a blue spruce. In the city, snow was something to be scraped off, scooped up, and thrown away. It was cursed at by driver and pedestrian alike and quickly lost its white purity to become soot-smudged and as grey as soiled laundry. But outside this window, the snow lay in protected majesty within the boundaries of a rustic split-rail fence—an expanse of pure white laid down by Jack Frost and untouched by pollution or human hands.

A slow smile curved Ashley's mouth. *Untouched by human hands.* What a perfect opportunity! She was on vacation and weren't vacations meant for play? She hadn't played in snow since she was in college.

Five minutes later—bundled up in a red ski jacket and furlined snow boots with a red stocking cap pulled over her head—she was rolling an ever-growing ball of snow across the yard. The snow was just wet enough to stick well. By the time Ashley finished pushing black rocks in place for the eyes, a nose, and a wide half-moon grin, it was nearly noon.

She stepped back to look at her creation and laughed. Mr. Snowman was a trifle lopsided and one eye was bigger than the other, but he grinned merrily back at her.

The rumble of a powerful engine reached her

ears and Ashley turned to see J.D.'s silver four-wheel drive pickup approaching down the lane that led from the ranch buildings to the highway. She waved and crossed the lawn to the gate when he braked and stopped in front of the house.

Ashley's heart gave an odd leap as she watched him slide out from behind the wheel. The sheepskin jacket stretched over broad shoulders, his long legs encased in blue jeans, black stetson tugged low over his brow. His black gaze ran over her and she smiled, a strange glow of delight filling her.

J.D. took in the tousled sable hair and rosy cheeks beneath the red cap. Snow clung to her gloves, boots, and jeans. She radiated health and happiness, and his heart lurched at the welcome glow that lit her golden eyes. Was that just for him? Or was she so bored that she would have been ecstatically happy to see any one?

"Hi," she said, smiling into black eyes. Was she wrong, or did those ebony depths lighten and warm?

"Hi," he responded, an answering smile curving the hard line of his mouth. Somehow, he managed to pull his gaze away from her rosy cheeks and soft lips to look behind her. "What's this?"

"A snowman," she answered, grinning saucily back at him. "Isn't he cute?"

J.D. stared at the fat, lopsided creature.

"Yeah, cute." He tilted his head to one side, as if to get a better perspective. "Looks a little drunk, maybe, but definitely cute."

Ashley laughed.

"He's not drunk, I'm just a little out of practice. He's my first snowman since college." J.D. focused intently on her face and Ashley shifted self-consciously. He didn't say anything and she brushed a strand of silky hair away from her cheek. "It's nearly lunchtime. Did you come home for lunch?"

"Lunch?" he said slowly, seeming to have difficulty registering her question. His eyes left her face and he tugged his hat lower. "No," he said, turning to walk around the back of the house to the porch off the kitchen. Ashley followed him. "No, I don't want food."

Ashley stared at his broad back. There was something strange about the almost absent way he spoke. And he was walking slowly, as if he were concentrating on placing one foot in front of the other. Concerned, she hurried after him, letting the door slam shut and quickly unzipping and pulling off her wet boots before following him into the kitchen.

But he wasn't there. Damp boot prints marched across the kitchen's green-and-white linoleum and disappeared through the swinging door into the dining room. She pushed open the door and heard him slowly climbing the stairs. It sounded as if his body was hitting the wall as he climbed. Soft thuds joined the noise of boots on the stairs.

A frisson of concern raced up her spine. *Was he hurt?* She ran after him; tugging off gloves, hat, and jacket and dropping them. The door to his bedroom stood open and she ran quickly down the hallway and stepped inside, her anxious gaze searching for J.D.

He was sprawled on his back on top of the wide bed. Ashley ran across the room and bent over him. His thick, black lashes lay against the hard bones of his cheeks. It appeared that he had made it as far as the bed and then passed out. The fall knocked his hat off and his hair fell across his brow. Ashley smoothed it back off his forehead and her fingers encountered the dampness of cold sweat against hot skin.

Quickly, she tested his cheeks with the back of her fingers. He was hot, burning up with fever that singed color across his cheekbones. The hard mouth was relaxed and sweat beaded his upper lip.

Ashley was scared. What was wrong with him? How could he be so ill so quickly? She smoothed a shaky hand across his cheek. He seemed perfectly well last night!

"J.D.," she murmured, but there was no response. "J.D.! J.D.!" she said loudly, more strongly, one hand lightly tapping his cheek.

He stirred and muttered something unintelligible. Ashley was nearly in tears.

"Please, J.D.! Wake up!"

The thick lashes stirred, lifted over bemused black eyes. He struggled to focus on the worried face hovering over him.

"Ashley," he muttered. "Don't worry. This happens all the time. Pills—get the pills."

"What pills, J.D.?" she asked anxiously as his eyes started to drift closed again. "Where are they?"

"Bathroom cabinet," he managed to get out.

"I'll get them—I'll be right back."

She ran down the hall to the bathroom and flung open the medicine cabinet.

"Pills, pills," she said to herself, shifting aside deodorant, mouthwash, Band-Aids, and toothpaste before she found a small prescription bottle. She grabbed it and quickly read the label. "Take two tablets every four hours for fever until temperature is normal."

She was halfway out of the bathroom before she remembered water. She retraced her steps and filled a glass, her hand shaking and spilling it across her fingers as she ran back to J.D.'s bedroom. He lay just as she had left him—eyes closed, hard features pale.

She set the pills and water down on the bedside table and leaned over J.D. once more.

"J.D.," she called with soft urgency.

The thick lashes stirred against cheeks flushed

with fever. They lifted to reveal black eyes again struggling to focus.

J.D. heard Ashley's voice and recognized the worry in the soft tones. His head felt light as air, floating above his leaden body that alternately burned with heat and shook with chills. He knew what was wrong with him; he recognized all the signs. He should have left the South Pasture earlier, when lightheadedness, blurred vision, and the rising fever first hit him. But he wanted to finish checking the fences. The recurring jungle fever was a souvenir of his tour of duty in Vietnam. It attacked infrequently, but always with the same warning signs. He should have recognized them immediately. As it was, he was in for several days of discomfort and drifting in and out of consciousness.

He forced his eyes open, fighting to lift his heavy lids. Once open, the world within his vision spun in a vortex of bright darts of light with slowly closing darkness at the edges. He forced himself to concentrate and finally Ashley's worried face came into focus. She was bent over him, thick hair falling forward and brushing against his cheek with scented enticement. Her fingers were soft against his face; cool against feverishly hot skin.

He tried to speak, but his vocal cords seemed strangely reluctant to work—lethargic and slow, rusty and thick. He managed, however, to force the words out past an unwilling voice box.

"Pills," he rasped and Ashley's hair brushed

his mouth as she nodded. Moments later, she was lifting his head. He swallowed the two small, yellow tablets and sipped water from the glass she held to his lips. He needed to tell her something, but he couldn't remember what. Damn! Fiercely he concentrated, the force of his will twisting his face into a frown.

"J.D.," Ashley said anxiously, afraid of the frown that carved deep lines between his black brows. "Are you in pain? What is it?"

J.D. remembered. And once again forced his voice to work.

"Call Joanne—she knows what to do."

It was all he could get out. The hovering blackness closed over him and he fell into its demanding darkness, floating and falling with no control, with no ability to impose his strong will to demand his release.

"J.D.! J.D.!"

He didn't respond to Ashley's urging. Frantically, she bit her lip and drew a deep breath to calm her racing heartbeat.

Joanne—he told me to call Joanne!

A telephone stood on the nightstand and Ashley dialed Joanne's number with trembling fingers.

"Hello?" Joanne's bubbly voice was a calm port in Ashley's storm.

"Joanne—thank God!"

"Ashley?" Joanne's voice lost its cheery bounce and changed to quick concern. "What is it?"

"It's J.D. He's sick—he's burning up with fever and now he won't answer me. I think he's unconscious, but before he passed out he told me to call you." The words tumbled out one over another and before Ashley could draw breath, Joanne's calm voice interrupted her.

"Calm down, Ashley, you're talking so fast I can't understand you. Now say that again. There's something wrong with J.D.?"

Ashley drew a deep breath, willed her voice to stop shaking, and concentrated on speaking concisely.

"J.D. came home about ten minutes ago, walked straight into the house and upstairs to his room where he passed out on his bed. But before he lost consciousness, he had me get some prescription tablets from the bathroom and told me to call you." Anxiety laced Ashley's voice. "What is it, Joanne? What's wrong with him? His skin feels so hot—he's burning up."

"He must be having another bout of the jungle fever he picked up in Vietnam," Joanne replied. "You say he took the prescription medicine?"

"Yes, just before he passed out."

"That's good. The sooner the medicine gets into his system, the better."

"Should I call his doctor? Or an ambulance? Or—"

"No, no," Joanne said soothingly. "None of those things. There really isn't anything a doctor can do for him, except give him medication and you've already done that. J.D. keeps the prescription in the house all the time because he never knows when he'll have an attack. I don't think he's been bothered with it for over a year.''

"But there must be something I can do. He seems so sick.''

"Of course there is. Keep him as comfortable a possible. Get as much liquid and juices down him as you can and sponge him off to keep the fever down.''

"How long will he be like this?''

"The attacks usually last for a few days, but J.D. is so stubborn—he's always up and out when he's still so weak he can barely stay on his horse!''

Reassured by Joanne's calm knowledge of J.D.'s illness, Ashley thanked her and rang off. Nevertheless, the receiver clattered against the telephone, her fingers still trembling.

Ashley eyed J.D.

Joanne said to make you comfortable, she said silently, her amber gaze sliding over his long length. He looked singularly uncomfortable, still dressed in his heavy denim jacket with his long blue-jeaned legs bent at the knee and angled over the edge of the bed. As she watched, he mumbled unintelligibly and turned his head restlessly.

Well, she decided with determination. *First things first*.

She lifted up one booted foot and tugged on the scuffed black heel. The boot barely moved. Re-

WINTERFIRE / 83

membering a scene from an old western movie, she straddled his leg with her back to him and tugged again. It moved more readily, but by the time she had both of his boots off, she was disheveled and huffing and puffing. With her hands on her hips, she looked down at him and contemplated her next move.

"The jacket," she muttered to herself.

Getting him extricated from his jacket was no small feat. He was a big man and the thick sheepskin stubbornly refused to slide off easily. With great effort, she finally got him out of it. She blew her hair out of her eyes before unbuttoning his blue-flannel shirt and button-front thermal undershirt. She spread the shirts open and froze, her throat going dry. A mat of black curls arrowed down his broad chest to disappear beneath the waistband of his jeans. He groaned and shifted on the bed. The powerful muscles that ridged his ribs rippled, drawing Ashley's fascinated gaze downward to follow the path of black curls until they narrowed to circle his navel and become a thin line.

Without thinking, Ashley stretched out a finger and traced his belly button. His skin—brown silk roughened by black hair—was warm to her touch. With difficulty, Ashley pulled her thoughts from the pleasure of just looking and touching and forced herself to concentrate on getting him out of his shirts.

No matter how she tried to avoid it, the maneuverings necessary to remove the garments forced her into close contact with him. Her nose was buried against the hard muscles that started below his collarbone and her arms stretched around him while she tugged at the stubborn shirts. As she tried to pull J.D.'s limp body toward her to release them, he mumbled incoherently and his arms slid around her, trapping her against him.

She couldn't understand what he was saying, partly because he was mumbling and partly because her senses were on overload. Each breath she drew caught the heady scent of musky male combined with traces of aftershave and just a hint of smoke. The silky black chest hairs tickled her nose and brushed her cheek when she turned her face sideways.

That was a mistake: She had an unobstructed view of a flat brown disk within a swirl of black curls. As she stared in fascination, it peaked as if brushed by a chill wind. Quickly, she tilted her face upward to search his face and found his eyes open, the black gaze glittering hotly as it met hers.

The hard arms tightened, one hand sliding up between her shoulder blades and across her nape to catch her hair. With a quick twist, the ponytail holder was gone and his fingers fastened themselves in the thick mane of sable silk to hold her still.

"You have the most beautiful mouth," he muttered feverishly. His gaze sought her face and fastened on the curve of her lips. "I've wanted to taste it ever since I looked up and saw you in that bar's mirror. Come here."

He shifted, pulling her higher as his black head bent lower. Before Ashley could protest, his lips bit softly at hers. Hot and dry with the fever that raged in his body, his mouth moved caressingly over hers, brushing the soft skin at the corners, the point of her chin, the tip of her nose in slow, tasting movements until it settled over her lips in a devastatingly masculine possession that was totally out of Ashley's experience.

She knew he was ill. She knew he probably wasn't aware of what he was doing. Somewhere in the back of her fogged brain she dimly knew that she should be struggling to stop him, but his un-complicated, straightforward passion was over-whelmingly compelling. Used to men wanting her only as a status symbol, she was unable to resist the seductive, blatant male need that tautened the muscular body against which his arms crushed her. Ashley went under in a haze of arousal with barely a murmur of protest.

His mouth twisted demandingly over hers and when her lips parted, his tongue moved forcefully into the warm, wet hollow he sought. A groan of heated pleasure reached Ashley's dazed hearing as she tried to cope with the shocking things he was doing and the flood of hot sensations that swept through her body. She was acutely sensitive to the crush of his muscles against her soft curves, the faintly raspy stroke of his tongue against the sleek wetness of the soft inner skin of her mouth.

Just when she thought she would faint with pleasure, the pressure of his mouth lessened, the fingers wound in her hair relaxed their grip. The hard body she was pressed against tensed, muscles tightening in refusal. Ashley felt rather than heard his grunt of protest as he lost his struggle for consciousness, his arms sliding reluctantly from around her.

Ashley forced her trembling arms to prop herself up and push away from J.D. Shaky fingers rested against lips reddened from the warm pressure of his hard mouth. She shoved the tousled mane of hair back from her face and drew a shaky breath, staring down at J.D.'s hard face. Belatedly, she realized that one hand still rested on his bare chest, black curls twining around the pale, slim fingers that lay against the brown skin.

She snatched her fingers from the seductive warmth of skin and male muscles, her flushed skin burning even hotter as she realized that she was staring hungrily at his body. He was beautifully made, with broad shoulders that tapered down to a chest defined by the ripple and flow of muscles to a narrow waist. His ribs and flat stomach were delineated by a washboard of muscled flesh.

One of his hands lay palm up near her hip and

Ashley slipped her hand inside his cupped palm, her fingertips tracing the hard callouses. He'd gotten that beautifully muscled torso from hard work, not from exercising in a trendy gym, and Ashley felt a fierce surge of pride that nearly overwhelmed her. It was a foreign emotion, but one she recognized immediately as a primal delight in his male strength.

Far from being repelled by J.D.'s mouth on hers, Ashley had revelled in it. And she was completely enthralled by everything about this man that lay unconscious on the big bed. The situation was so extraordinary that Ashley could barely believe it was happening. She'd long ago accepted her own lack of interest in a physical relationship, although she hadn't given up dreaming of romance. To have her dreams come true so unexpectedly was startling. And if his words and actions meant anything, he was attracted to her, too.

Ashley forced herself to stand. She had to stop daydreaming over him and finish undressing him. Fortunately, he'd rolled to one side and shifted off the shirts and Ashley picked them up and dropped them atop the jacket on the floor.

She eyed his nearly stripped body with misgivings and decided to leave his jeans on him. Even though she was sure he would be more comfortable without them, she couldn't bring herself to unzip the denim and slide the worn fabric down those long legs. She lifted his dark head to slide a pillow underneath it, enjoying the feel of his silky black hair caught beneath her fingers as she eased him down onto the cool white pillowcase. She found a light blanket on a closet shelf and spread it across his waist and legs.

Joanne said to sponge him off, she remembered. The thought of running a cool cloth over him didn't sound clinical at all. Instead, it stirred warm butterflies of anticipation in her stomach. *Enough of that*, Ashley ordered herself sternly, *the man's ill*.

All her admonishments were forgotten later, however, as she stroked a damp cloth over the hard bones of his face, which was somehow younger and more vulnerable in repose with thick lashes and eyelids shuttering those fierce black eyes. With a mental shrug, Ashley stopped berating herself and simply enjoyed running the cloth over the satiny smooth brown skin covering the bulging biceps and the ripple of chest muscles.

J.D. swam upward through darkness thick as black molasses. It clung to him, dragged at his struggling senses, until it reluctantly gave up and thinned to grey fog. Suddenly, he realized three things. He was burning up with heat. His throat felt like parched desert sand. And he needed to visit the bathroom. Now. Immediately.

He managed to lift eyelids that felt weighted down by anvils and shove away the blanket. He swung his feet over the edge of the bed and sat up, resting his aching head on his palms while he fought against the overwhelming dizziness that attacked him with a vengeance.

His grunt of pain awoke the woman curled up in the rocking chair next to the oak nightstand.

"What is it? Are you in pain?" Anxiety sounded in her sleepy tone.

J.D. cautiously swung his head to the right and his surprised gaze found Ashley. Her tousled hair and rumpled clothing clearly indicated that she had been there for some time. What his aching brain couldn't understand was why?

"What are you doing here?" he demanded, his deep voice rough with sleep. The effort set off a gong inside his head and a frown of pain drew together his black brows.

"Watching over you, of course." Ashley ignored his testy tone and slid her cool fingers over his forehead. "It's time for another tablet."

"Later, honey." J.D.'s fingers closed over her wrist and moved her hand away from his face. He pushed up and off the bed and cursed softly at the weakness that invaded his limbs and made him sway with dizziness.

"What are you doing? You shouldn't be out of bed?"

"I'm going to the bathroom," he growled, his tone daring her to argue with him.

"Oh." Nonplussed, she stared up into the black

eyes just barely visible through the narrowed fringe of lashes. "Okay."

The wry grin that briefly twisted the hard mouth underlined the ludicrousness of her permission before he took a step forward and staggered to the right.

"Be careful!"

Ashley slipped a hand around his waist and slid under his unresisting arm, tucking her shoulder securely beneath his.

"Lean on me," she commanded.

J.D. was amazed at the sturdy strength contained in that soft, curved body. He was also amazed at how aware his own aching body was of those same soft curves. Their position forced them into contact from shoulder to thigh, and his temperature shot up several degrees—a rise he couldn't blame on the jungle fever.

Just as she was about to ease through the bathroom doorway with him, J.D. stopped her with one big hand planted firmly on the slim curve of her shoulder.

"This is as far as you go."

"But what if you fall?"

"I won't fall."

Suddenly aware of where they were, Ashley flushed deeply and stepped back. Her quick movement forced his hand from her shoulder and down over the beginning slope of one full breast before she was free of his touch.

She gestured vaguely toward the wall beside the white bathroom door.

"I, uhmmm—I'll wait out here. If you need me, just call."

His black gaze was unreadable and stayed fixed on her red face as the door slowly closed, easing her from view.

Ashley's anxious ears heard only the sound of running water from the bathroom and she was relieved when the door swung open and J.D. stepped out into the hall. Without asking, she pulled his arm back over her shoulders, snuggled against his side, helped him back down the hall, and eased him back onto his bed.

His head was pounding and J.D. lifted a hand to hold it. He frowned at his bare arm. Something wasn't quite right here. He stared at his naked chest and bootless feet.

He lifted his head slowly and eyed Ashley's slim form. Her back was to him as she took two tablets out of the bottle and poured a glass of water from a pitcher. The circle of lamplight enfolded her and struck glints of gold-fire in her tumbled hair.

Ashley turned, glass and tablets in her hands, and was halted by J.D.'s narrow-eyed black stare.

"What's the matter?"

"My clothes," he said slowly. "Who took them off?"

Ashley could feel the heated flush move up her throat and cheeks.

"I did," she said with as much calm as she could muster.

"You did," he repeated slowly. He continued to stare at her in silence. "I don't remember."

"You passed out right after you took the first tablets and told me to call Joanne. She explained what was wrong and told me to make you comfortable, so I took your shirt and boots off."

He continued to stare at her, a vaguely confused look in his black eyes, while he groped for an elusive memory.

"I seem to remember walking upstairs, but then—" His gaze flashed to her face and searched it before fastening on the soft curve of her mouth. "I either had one hell of a dream or I made a pass at you," he said softly.

FIVE

He remembers!

Ashley's whole body heated with embarrassment.

J.D.'s aching body tensed at the sight of the revealing pink that moved up her throat and colored her face.

"I made a pass at you," he confirmed with resignation.

Ashley didn't respond. She couldn't. Her voice seemed to be stuck somewhere between her stomach and her throat.

"Damn! Look at me," he ordered softly, trying to ignore the throbbing in his head, and waited patiently until she raised a wary gold gaze to meet his. "I'm sorry. The only excuse I can offer is that

I was out of my head with fever, or I would never have touched you.''

Each word he uttered stabbed a needle of sharp pain into Ashley's sensitive dreamworld. He was sorry he'd kissed her! What had been sheer pleasure for her clearly hadn't been for him.

"That's perfectly all right," she said stiffly, forcing the words out through a throat tight with frozen tears. "I'm sure that if you had known what you were doing you wouldn't have kissed me."

Even a blind man could see he'd hurt her feelings, J.D. thought with disgust. And she'd leapt to a conclusion that was light years from the truth. His head hurt too damned much to think of a polite way out of the tangled mess he'd made of his apology. So he settled for the truth.

"That's a lie, honey," he said bluntly. "The plain truth is that whether I'm conscious or unconscious I want to do a lot more than kiss you. I want you in my bed. Badly. It's taken all my will power to keep my hands off you. But that doesn't excuse my grabbing you, even if I was out of my head with fever.''

Ashley was dumbfounded. And exhilarated. And completely bewildered.

"That's all right," she managed to get out. "You didn't know what you were doing. And besides, it was only a kiss.''

J.D. bit off a curse and glared at her.

"If you kiss every man like that, no wonder they try to paw you and then get mad when you won't follow through."

The soft flush of color faded from Ashley's face, leaving her pale and stricken, her golden eyes wounded as they stared down into his.

"I don't kiss every man like I kissed you," she said with quiet dignity, her hand gripping the glass of water. "I've never before kissed anyone like that. I've never wanted to."

A fierce swell of joy shook J.D. He reached out a hand to claim her, to pull her close, and at the last moment barely managed to just caress her fingers, which still clutched the glass.

"You shouldn't tell me things like that," he said huskily. "Especially not when we're alone in my bedroom. And besides," he added, pain and regret flickering briefly in his black eyes, "I'm not a man you should feel that way about."

"Why not?" Ashley asked bravely, watching the emotions move across the hard planes of his face.

"Because we're worlds apart, you and I," he responded. "I'm a man who neither trusts nor likes women. Especially city women. It's a lesson I learned long ago and I'm too old to unlearn it now. I have only one use for women and that's in bed. From what you've told me, I don't think you'd be interested in sharing my bed. And don't kid yourself that we couldn't end up in bed, honey. There's enough chemistry between us to light dynamite, and if we ever made love we'd burn each other up. I don't want you hurt, Joanne would never forgive me, and I'm not all that sure of my control where you're concerned," he said bluntly. "So don't tease me. You're liable to start something neither of us can stop."

Ashley stared at him, fascinated by the images his words conjured up. Her gold eyes turned lambent, full lips parting with unconscious yearning, as her gaze dropped to his mouth.

J.D. unerringly read her thoughts.

"Stop looking at me like that," he said gruffly. "Unless you want me to strip you out of that sweater and jeans and take you right now."

Shocked, Ashley met his hot black stare with instant trepidation. "You're ill. You couldn't—"

J.D. bit off a curse.

"It wouldn't matter if I was on my deathbed. You make me so hot I could make love to you if I was unconscious. I told you—don't tease me. If you keep looking at me wondering what it would be like to be under me, I'll show you. Do you understand?"

"I understand."

"You do?" J.D. gave her an enigmatic look. "I'm glad you do because I'm not at all sure I understand why I have to want someone like you till I ache.''

Affronted, Ashley glared at him.

''What do you mean—someone like me! What's wrong with me?''

''Physically, nothing. You're perfect. You've got a body that makes mine ache just to look at it, a face out of every man's dream, a voice that makes men think of satin sheets and hot nights.''

Ashley was suffused with warmth. Heat pooled in her belly and shifted even lower. He was seducing her with words and it took an effort to concentrate on what he *wasn't* saying.

''And that's wrong?''

''No, that's not wrong,'' he growled in irritation. ''It's the rest of you that's wrong!''

Ashley stared at him blankly. ''The rest of me?''

''Yeah, the rest of you. The part that lives in New York City in an expensive apartment, wears mink coats and diamond studded wristwatches, and jets in and out of her friends' lives every couple of years.''

His sarcasm cut Ashley to the bone.

''I told you before that I don't live in the fast lane,'' she said. ''And the mink and the wristwatch were gifts from companies after I modeled them.''

J.D. stared at her, his hard face unreadable. He'd hurt her again. And if the truth were known, it was really his ex-fiancée he was describing, not

Ashley. Karla wouldn't have spent the night curled up in the rocking chair just so she could watch over him. No, Karla would have caught the next plane back to the bright lights and the next party. Just the way she did when he was shipped back from 'Nam, his face scarred and his leg so badly damaged the doctors weren't sure he'd walk again. He could barely remember what she looked like after all these years, but her carelessly cruel words were imprinted on his brain: "*I know you'll understand, J.D. No woman wants to live with a cripple. I just couldn't do it and trying would only make it worse. Far better that we make the break now instead of later.*" Then she turned and walked out the door, leaving him with wounds that dug far deeper than the shrapnel that scarred his face and thigh.

"If I'm wrong, I apologize." He managed abruptly, his black gaze turning away from the wounded gold eyes.

He pushed up off the bed and unsnapped his jeans.

"Turn around," he said gently as Ashley continued to stare at him, confused by his switch from angry bitterness to quiet gentleness.

Her gaze flashed to his hands where they rested on his jeans, thumbs hooked inside the worn denim.

"Oh!"

He smiled at her flush of embarrassment as she quickly spun around.

Ashley heard the whisper of denim sliding against his skin and the rustle of covers followed by the slight creak of bedsprings.

"You can turn around now."

She drew a steadying breath and schooled her face into calm lines before she turned to face him. Her heart lurched at the sight of his black hair against the white pillowcase and the sheets turned down below the broad expanse of tan chest.

"You need to take your pills before you fall back to sleep."

The effort seemed to have exhausted him. Ashley gently stroked a cool cloth over his temples and forehead.

"You don't have to stay," he mumbled, his dark gaze meeting hers as she bent over him. He couldn't tell her how good it felt to have someone care, or how infinitely comforting the touch of her hand was as it smoothed the cool, damp cloth over his hot skin.

"I know. I want to," she said quietly, a small, warm smile curving her lips.

"You really do have the most beautiful mouth I've ever seen," he muttered. The thick lashes drifted together and he slept.

An insistent hammering sound woke Ashley the next morning. Sunlight was streaming through the windows and falling across her face. Reluctantly, she sat upright in the rocking chair, wincing at the stab of pain in her neck. She massaged it, yawning and acknowledging that sleeping curled like a pretzel in a chair was not the most comfortable way to spend a night.

The pounding sound stopped momentarily, then resumed, and Ashley realized that someone was at the door. She unwound the blanket and jumped out of the chair, hurrying across the room and down the hallway and stairs.

The lanky cowboy, who was just about to knock again, stared openmouthed at the dishevelled woman who swung the door open. Sable hair tumbled around a face bare of makeup. Her gold eyes were still sleepy but inquiring, their color echoed in the loose sweater that bloused over slim jeans. Small feet with toes tipped in Fire Engine Red polish curled against the cool oak flooring.

"Yes?" the slightly husky voice asked musically.

Ace Langan, J.D.'s foreman for fifteen years, was nearly speechless at finding a woman in his boss's house. He swallowed noisily and pulled the hat off his thinning grey hair.

"Unhhh—I, umm—who are you?" he burst out, so nonplussed that he completely forgot any semblance of politeness.

"I'm Ashley Tierney," Ashley responded, more than a bit taken aback at his abruptness. "Who are you?"

"The name's Ace, ma'am, Ace Langan. I'm the foreman here."

"Oh, I see," Ashley responded.

The two stood staring at each other for a moment.

"I reckon you must be a friend of Miss Stefanie's?"

"I'm afraid I don't know a Miss Stefanie. Oh, is that J.D.'s sister?" At Ace's nod of confirmation, Ashley shook her head. "No, I don't know her. I'm a friend of Joanne's."

"Oh." None of this made sense to Ace and he decided to try another tack.

"Unhhh—I was lookin' for the boss—"

"If you mean J.D., he's ill and can't be disturbed," Ashley responded, hugging her arms around her to fend off the cold air.

"He's sick, is he? What's wrong with him?"

"Some sort of fever, evidently he's had it before. Joanne said he picked it up in Vietnam."

"If he's got a ragin' fever and he's passin' out a lot, that's it all right," Ace concurred sagely and eyed Ashley with interest. "Well, I reckon I'll get back to work then. When J.D. wakes up, you might tell him that me and the boys will keep things goin' till he's up and about."

"I'll tell him," Ashley smiled at the lanky cowboy and started to close the door.

"You're a friend of Joanne's, eh?" The curious Ace couldn't resist one last probe for information.

"Yes, a college friend," Ashley answered with a smile as she gently closed the door. "Bye."

"Bye." Ace gave up and clumped across the porch and down the steps to the snowy path.

Ashley closed the door and pulled aside the sheer curtain to peer out the window and watch the lanky figure amble over to the small cottages that housed the cowboys.

A mischievous smile curved her lips and sparkled in her gold eyes. He'd been so obviously eaten up with curiosity. What kind of man was J.D. McCullough that his employee was actually shocked to see a woman in his house? She liked the idea that she was the only woman J.D. was seeing, even if it was just because he was doing Joanne a favor. J.D. seemed to have some faulty, stubborn conceptions about why they were incompatible, but there was no way, Ashley decided, that she was going to let him off the hook that easily. Especially not since he had admitted he was attracted to her. And not when he was the first man in all her life who made her knees weak and her head spin.

Ashley's determination to charm the elusive rancher underwent a severe testing in the next three days. At first, J.D. was either burning up with fever and rambling in delirium, or sleeping. But then the medicine began to work and he became perfectly lucid—and grouchy.

When he growled at her because the soup was too hot, Ashley lost her will to be sweet and considerate. With her small fists planted on her hips, she matched him glare for glare, her gold eyes shooting sparks.

"J.D. McCullough, you're going out of your way to be contrary and impossible. And I'm telling you right now, you can just stop it because I'm staying right where I am until you're back on your feet."

"Oh, you are, are you?" he growled back, noticing how her breasts lifted with each indignant breath, straining the buttons on the emerald-green silk blouse. "Why?"

"Because whether you'll admit it or not, you need someone to look after you and I happen to be the one who's here," she paused, mischief replacing exasperation in her gold eyes, "and because I want you to kiss me again when you're perfectly well and can't blame it on being delirious, that's why!"

J.D.'s frown was replaced with astonishment. For a long moment he stared at her speechlessly. Then the thick, black lashes narrowed over night-dark eyes.

"I warned you about teasing me," he began threateningly, but Ashley interrupted him.

"I know you did," she agreed, smiling openly now, "but I figure I'm safe for a few days more."

"I wouldn't bet on it," he growled, but an unwilling smile tugged at the corners of his mouth. "You're enjoying this, aren't you?" he murmured, amused.

"What?" Ashley's eyes widened innocently, but the sparkle of mischief in their gold depths gave her away.

"Bossing me around while I'm damn near helpless in bed," he said, a teasing note in his deep voice.

"Hah!" she retorted. "Fat lot of good it does me! All you do is growl and complain! Either the soup is too hot or too cold. Or the lamp is too dim or too bright! Or the—"

"All right, all right," he conceded a bit shamefacedly. "I make a lousy patient. I *hate* being sick."

Ashley rolled her eyes. "Oh! I would have *never* guessed."

"You have a smart mouth," he shot back.

Ashley wiggled expressive brows at him and he grinned, not a brief twitch of the lips but a real grin. She smiled back at him, and for a moment a warm rapport bound them together in a sunny cocoon. But J.D. soon broke the web that held them, tearing his gaze from hers.

Ashley drew a deep breath and linked her hands tightly together in front of her, casting about for something to break the suddenly tense silence.

"It's only three days till Christmas," she said brightly, "and you haven't been able to put up your tree, what with being ill and all. Would you like me to have one of the cowboys get one for you?"

J.D. stared at her as if she had suddenly grown two heads.

"A tree," he said blankly. "What for?"

"To decorate, of course."

J.D. continued to stare at her with confusion.

"You know—a Christmas tree. The kind you drag into your living room, put into a stand, string colored lights on, hang ornaments all over, stack packages with ribbons and bows under." Ashley planted her hands on her hips and eyed him wryly. "The kind your mother and father used to have perhaps?"

"Oh." J.D. grunted and tucked the sheet under his arms and punched the pillow higher beneath his black head.

Ashley waited patiently, but he didn't say anything else.

"Well, do you want me to?"

"Do I want you to do what?"

Ashley let out a frustrated sigh.

"Do you want me to get you a tree?"

"I don't put up Christmas trees."

"Why not?"

"I just don't, that's all."

"Nobody just doesn't put up a Christmas tree." Ashley glared at him. "Nearly everyone I know has a Christmas tree. It's, it's—un-American not to have a Christmas tree."

"Yeah? Well, then I guess I'm un-American," he said stubbornly.

"Why not?"

J.D. didn't even bother to respond.

"You heard me," she said persistently. "Why not? Don't you have any Christmas spirit?"

"Of course, I do! You make me sound like some sort of Scrooge, for pete's sake! I just don't see the point in cutting down a tree, dragging it into the house, and spending a couple of hours hanging stuff on it. Who's going to see it anyway? Then, in a couple of weeks, I just have to take all the decorations off, put them away, and drag the tree back outside. It's a waste of a perfectly good tree and a waste of my time!"

Ashley stared at him. His words painted a stark picture of a man living alone with no one to share the simple joys of the holiday season. She couldn't help comparing it with her own love of Christmas, and the time and care she spent on decorating her apartment each December.

She decided to try a different approach.

"But, J.D., I probably won't be able to go to Joanne's for Christmas Day and it just doesn't seem like the holiday season without a tree. Would you mind terribly if I put one up?"

J.D.'s black gaze ran over the soft, hopeful face. He couldn't hold out against her little-girl eagerness. He wasn't even sure he wanted to anymore.

"All right, all right," he growled, attempting to conceal that his usual indifference to women's pleas had turned to mush when faced with the overwhelming urge to see this woman smile again.

Her face lit up like the Christmas tree she wanted and she impulsively bent to brush her soft lips against his cheek.

"Thank you!" she bubbled, oblivious to his reaction to her soft touch. "I'll ask Ace to cut one for us tomorrow."

"I'll tell him," J.D. said decisively. Ace was going to think he'd gone soft in the head as it was. J.D. didn't want the gossipy foreman pumping Ashley for more information.

Ashley had been content with J.D.'s cooperation, but when Ace rapped on the front door at six A.M. the following morning, she was dismayed to see J.D. descending the stairs fully dressed.

"Where are you going?"

"Back to work."

"But you can't! It's too soon!"

J.D.'s hard face softened as the worried face with its golden gaze focused anxiously on his.

"You worry too much," he said gruffly and stretched out a calloused forefinger to smooth the frown wrinkles from between the soft arch of her sable brows. The simple, brief contact jolted him to his boots and he hastily pulled his hand back. Ashley felt something, too. Her golden gaze heated with unconscious longing.

Abruptly, he turned away and yanked open the

front door. Ace's laconic face split with a welcoming grin.

"Mornin', boss. Good to see you up and about again."

J.D. grunted a reply and stepped across the threshold.

Ashley stood in the doorway. "J.D.," she called as the two men descended the porch steps to the snowy walkway. They turned and looked back at her. "Don't forget the tree!"

J.D. paused. Dressed in narrow-leg blue jeans and a loose red wool pullover, her slim figure was framed in the doorway. Her dark hair was a tousled mass of silk around her face and across her shoulders; her face bare and freshly innocent without makeup. He felt the same strong emotion that had swamped him the night he stepped into the fragrant kitchen to find her humming to herself at the stove.

"I won't," his deep voice was rougher than usual and he cleared his throat self-consciously. He was just about to turn away when a thought occurred to him. "Would you like to go with us when we cut it down?"

Her face lit up with delight.

"I'd love to!"

"Fine," he said gruffly and turned away from her. "Be ready by ten o'clock. I should be back by then."

"I'll be ready. Bye!"

The door closed behind them and J.D. strode off down the sidewalk toward the gate. He pushed it open and glanced back to see Ace standing still, staring at him with a dumbstruck look on his creased face.

"Are you working today or are you going to stand there staring at me all morning?" he growled, glaring at his foreman.

Jarred out of his astonishment, Ace jerked into motion and clumped down the walk. J.D. rounded the truck and yanked open the driver's door.

Ace pulled open his own door and heaved himself up into the high cab. The big pickup truck's engine turned over with a throaty roar and J.D. shifted gears and set the truck in motion. Ace managed to control his curiosity for at least five minutes before it overwhelmed him.

"You're puttin' up a Christmas tree this year, are you?"

"Yeah," J.D. growled in response.

Ace eyed the big man, but J.D. said nothing further. Ace tried a different tack. "She's mighty pretty, that Ashley. And nice, too. Offered me coffee and pie the other morning when I came by. Best pie I've had in a dog's age—she sure can cook. Not hardly what you'd expect from a woman from New York City who does fancy modelin'," he added, watching J.D. out of the corner of his eye.

"Yeah."

"She just out here visitin', is she?" Ace probed with an innocently inquiring air.

"She's supposed to be visiting Joanne, but Cassie has the mumps. And she'll be going back to New York City right after Christmas." Before Ace could ask another question J.D. asked him how the stock in the South Pasture were faring and diverted, Ace answered. J.D. heaved a silent sigh of relief. He couldn't seem to stop himself from thinking about the woman. He didn't want to hear the garrulous Ace sing her praises all day long.

SIX

Ashley was ready and waiting by ten o'clock and when the silver pickup halted in front of the house, she ran down the walk.

Ace stepped out of the cab to let her in before swinging back onto the high seat and slamming the door. Ashley found herself pressed against J.D.'s side; her legs straddled the gear shift, his thigh warm against hers.

"Hi," she smiled up at him, scanning his face for any sign of fever and finding none. A quick, warm smile lit his face.

"Hi," he answered and faced forward to shift the big truck into gear. As he shifted, his fingers brushed Ashley's knees and inner thigh and his body went taut. *This is not a good idea,* he thought

111

grimly. He'd forgotten to take into consideration the cab's close quarters when he'd asked Ashley to go tree cutting with them. He was torn between being glad Ace was there to keep him from making a complete fool of himself, and wishing he would disappear in a flash of smoke so he could stop the truck, push Ashley down onto the seat, and kiss her senseless. Wanting to touch her and not being able to do anything about it was beginning to fray his nerves and shorten his temper.

He shot a glance at her, but she was asking Ace about the cattle in the feedlot next to the big barn. He swore silently. Clearly, she wasn't having the same problem he was having. If anything, she pressed closer when he tried to inch away from her soft thigh, which was glued to his.

Just then she shifted and looked at him, strands of dark hair catching on his coat sleeve as she turned. The gold eyes turned up to his were smokey, darkened with awareness. J.D.'s frustration lessened before she turned back to Ace. So, she wasn't immune to the press of their bodies after all!

Ashley struggled to keep her mind on what Ace was saying.

"Best place to cut trees is on the national forest land over there," he gestured ahead of them.

Ashley peered out the side window with interest. The rolling hills were steeper, the pine forests thickening and growing closer to the narrow road.

"J.D. leases grazing rights from the government on three-thousand acres of this land," Ace continued. " 'Course, we don't have any cattle in here now. We drive them up in the spring and bring them back down closer to the barns in the winter."

"It's beautiful up here," Ashley exclaimed, staring raptly at the Christmas-card perfection of stately pines frosted with snow and backed by majestic mountains.

"Yup," Ace said with pride. He cocked a grizzled brow at the entranced woman wedged between him and his boss. "Prettier than the city, ain't it?"

Ashley flashed him a teasing look and pretended to ponder his statement.

"I don't know, Ace. Central Park in winter is pretty, too, you know."

"Humph!" the old cowboy grunted. "Couldn't be nothin' prettier than Idaho mountains. No way!"

"You're right," Ashley said with a laugh. "I have to agree, I don't think I've ever seen anything prettier than this."

J.D. pulled the pickup off onto the narrow shoulder of the road and stopped.

"This looks like a good spot."

He shoved open the door and slid out. Ashley followed him quickly, sliding under the steering wheel and down onto the ground beside him. The snow crunched crisply beneath her boots, the air sharp and clear as she breathed deeply.

J.D. lifted a small chainsaw out of the truckbed, hefting it easily in big hands.

"See any you like?" J.D. asked.

The land dropped away in a gentle slope before leveling out into a small meadow dotted with trees in various stages of growth. Ashley narrowed her lashes to block out the glare of sunshine off the sparkling snow and slowly scanned the meadow in search of the perfect tree.

"That one looks good," she pointed halfway across the small meadow.

"Okay."

Ace rolled down the truck window and leaned out.

"Hey, boss," he called. "You won't need me, I'll just stay here and have a smoke."

"Sure, Ace," J.D. responded, hiding a grin at the old cowboy's heavy-handed attempt at matchmaking. Ace had persisted in grilling him all morning about Ashley and J.D. had been hard put to evade him. It was easy to see he was tickled pink that J.D. was on speaking terms with her.

He glanced over at Ashley just in time to see her sink up to her knees in snow in a ditch.

"Hey, wait a minute," he called. "Follow me so I can break a trail or you'll be covered with snow up to your waist."

Ashley was glad to follow in his tracks, although as soon as she climbed out of the ditch the snow only reached her boot tops. They crossed the meadow before J.D. stopped.

"Is this the one?"

Ashley walked up beside him to look at the tree. Up close, it was a bit lopsided with a bare spot on one side. She looked at J.D.

"What do you think?"

He squinted one eye and scrutinized the pine.

"I think somebody shaved that side."

Ashley laughed.

"I think you're right." She let her gaze roam over the trees just beyond them. "There's one that doesn't look too bad."

J.D. strode off across the snow, Ashley at his heels. But it, too, failed to pass Ashley's test for the perfect tree. Fifteen minutes later they had worked their way to the far edge of the meadow and were out of sight of the pickup. Ashley had rejected at least twelve trees along the way and J.D. was beginning to think this outing might take a lot longer than he had anticipated.

She lifted a hand to shade her eyes and searched the trees near her for possibilities.

"Christmas is only two days away," J.D. drawled with amusement. "You suppose we'll have a tree by then?"

Startled, Ashley looked up at him and laughed at the long-suffering look on his hard face.

"Perfect trees aren't found easily," she informed him loftily. "You have to have patience." Before he could reply, she spotted a tree just behind him. "Oh, look!" She grabbed his hand and tugged him after her, circling the tree with excitement. "This is it! Look, J.D., it's absolutely perfect!"

Privately, J.D. didn't think it looked a lot different from the last six trees they'd inspected, but he didn't want to push his luck.

"Absolutely perfect," he parroted. She gave him a sharp, doubtful look but he met her gaze with an innocent look. "Shall I cut it down?"

Ashley gave it one last tour of inspection before nodding her head in satisfaction.

"Yes, definitely. This is our tree."

"Great." J.D. yanked the starter cord on the chainsaw and its roar split the peaceful morning calm. "Stand back," he motioned Ashley away from the tree and in moments the graceful pine was crashing to the ground, sending up a flurry of snow.

J.D. shut off the saw and looked up at Ashley. The sight made him burst out laughing. She was covered in snow—from the top of her red knit cap, frosting the brown hair around her shoulders, down the front of her parka and jeans, all the way to her feet. She was looking at her snow sprayed body in total surprise and the bewilderment on her expressive face was priceless.

She heard him laughing and glanced up, her own laughter replacing shocked surprise.

"We look like snowmen!" she exclaimed.

"Yeah," J.D. chuckled—a deep rich sound that surprised him. He couldn't remember ever laughing this much before Ashley came into his life.

He put the chainsaw down by the felled tree and went to her in two long strides.

"I thought I told you to stand back," he commented, brushing snow from her sleeves.

"You did," she replied. "And I did—just not far enough."

She pulled off her gloves and brushed her cold fingers over his shoulders and the front of his snow-dusted jacket.

"I take it you've never cut down your own Christmas tree before?" he asked, busily wiping snow from her coat and hat.

"No, I always buy a tree from a lot." She brushed snow from his cheekbones and the arch of black brows.

J.D. went still, closing his eyes against the wash of pure pleasure at the feel of her fingers on his face. They slowed, stroking across the hard facial bones before sliding hesitantly into the thick, black hair above his ears.

He opened his eyes, a fierce hot black stare pinning hers as he slowly pulled off his gloves and let them drop. He slid his fingers into her hair, knocking off the red knit cap and letting it fall to the ground.

"Ashley," he said with aching need. His hands slowly closed over thick strands of her silken mane. "I want your mouth—I think I'd die to have it."

Already aroused, Ashley let her eyes drift shut and lifted her face to his. When his mouth closed over hers, it was with an abrupt, passionate heat that sent tremors quaking through her body. She'd wanted this, needed this. She tried to move closer to him but was frustrated by the bulky coats they wore. His nose was cold where it touched her cheek; his face and hair chilled beneath her fingers. But his mouth was hot, heating her and turning her body to fire beneath the slow pressure of his lips moving against hers with the greed of a starving man.

After long moments, he eased his mouth from hers to drag air into his lungs. His thumbs moved caressingly over the soft skin covering her cheekbones, one moving lower to stroke the outline of her mouth, which was faintly swollen from the long, hungry pressure of his kiss.

"Oh, baby," he sighed, leaning his forehead against hers. "What am I going to do about you? You shouldn't have let me kiss you. I've already warned you about the effect you have on me. Why didn't you stop me?"

"I didn't want to," she whispered, her warm breath feathering softly against his lips. "I wanted you to kiss me." Her liquid gaze moved with golden heat over the hard face nearly touching hers. "I liked it," she whispered huskily, too aroused to be shy. "Do it again."

J.D.'s hard body jerked as if he had been hit. He closed his eyes against the temptation. But Ashley moved the fraction of an inch necessary to touch his lips with hers and he was lost. He allowed her soft mouth to move tentatively, exploringly, against his for a moment before one of his arms slid around her waist and lifted her to him. His mouth nudged gently against hers, lifting to brush first one corner, then the other, before fitting carefully over hers again in a long, slow kiss.

At last, he lifted his warm mouth from hers. His black eyes blazed with emotion as they scanned her flushed, passionate face.

"You like it like that, don't you," he asked unsteadily. "Soft and slow."

"Yes," she murmured, helplessly returning his heated stare. "Do you?"

"Oh yeah," he breathed huskily. "I like it a lot. Maybe too much." He slowly lowered her to the ground, supporting her while she caught her breath and her legs steadied. Then he gently set her away from him and turned to pick up the chainsaw and the cut end of the tree trunk. He smiled a slow, devastating smile that accentuated his deep dimples. "I'm beginning to think you're a witch. You're damn sure addictive as hell!"

The warmly affectionate, teasing quality in his deep voice made the words a compliment, and Ashley shakily returned his smile and started ahead of him across the meadow.

When she climbed into the truck, Ace took one look at her faintly swollen mouth and began whistling, a pleased look on his weathered face.

He chatted amiably with Ashley on the drive back to the ranch, ignoring the fact that J.D. contributed little to the conversation and Ashley's comments were limited to yes or no responses.

"Why don't you drop me at the barns, J.D." He leaned forward around Ashley as J.D. negotiated the frozen ruts in the gravel lane leading to the ranch buildings. "I told Casey to shoe the big roan gelding and I want to make sure he did it right. That gelding is a mite fumble-footed if his shoes aren't just so."

J.D. nodded in agreement and drove past the house to pull up in front of the huge barn.

Ace tipped his Stetson and said a cheery, toothy good-bye to Ashley, slamming the pickup door behind him. J.D. eased his foot off the clutch and the big pickup moved forward smoothly, leaving a new set of snowy tracks in a broad half circle as they returned to park in front of the house.

When J.D. cut the motor, he looked down at Ashley's bent head. The silky fall of hair swung forward to hide her expression from him. She hadn't slid across the seat when Ace left and still sat pressed against his side. J.D. liked the feel of her warm, curved body tucked close against his. He liked it too much, he reflected with a silent groan. It would be too easy to get used to having her with him. And he couldn't forget that she would be returning to New York soon, leaving him behind. Alone. The thought was depressing and J.D. shoved it from his mind, yanked open the door, and slid out of the truck.

Startled by his abrupt departure, Ashley stared at him, her golden gaze faintly wary.

He read the wariness and instantly softened, his hard mouth lifting in a quick smile.

"Come on, little girl," he said, holding out a hand. "Let's wrestle your tree into the house."

Reassured, Ashley took his hand and allowed him to pull her out of the cab. J.D. let down the truck's tailgate and slid the tree out, balancing it easily over one broad shoulder. Ashley ran ahead of him up the sidewalk to hold the door open and then she closed it behind them.

The fragrance of pine filled the house. The smell meant Christmas and Ashley couldn't hold down a rising tide of excitement. Gold eyes sparkled as she stripped off jacket, hat, and gloves and hung them away in the hall closet.

"J.D.," she called, rubbing her cold hands together briskly as she walked into the living room where he knelt in front of the hearth in his shirtsleeves. He struck a match and lit the kindling beneath the fireplace logs. "Shall I make some hot coffee?"

J.D. glanced up to see her framed in the doorway. Her cheeks glowed pink from the cold, the gold eyes alive with delight as she looked at him. A sweet, painful ache hit him in the chest. Damn, she was pretty. He had to restrain the urge to cross the room and kiss her again.

"Sure," he managed to reply. "While you're doing that, I'll go up to the attic and bring down the boxes of Christmas stuff my folks used."

"Okay."

She smiled happily at him and left the room. J.D. gave a sigh of relief that he hadn't grabbed her when she passed him and left to climb the steps to the attic. When he came back into the room with his arms full of boxes, Ashley was just setting down a tray with mugs, a carafe of coffee, and a plate of ham sandwiches on a low oak drop-leaf table in front of the sofa.

J.D. stacked the boxes on the floor and dusted off his hands.

"They're covered with cobwebs; nobody's taken them out of the attic since Stef left and that's been over five years ago."

Ashley looked up from where she was pouring hot, black coffee into heavy mugs.

"Is Stef your sister?"

"Yeah, my little sister." J.D.'s face softened with affection. "She's eight years younger than me. She married a cattleman and moved to his ranch in western Montana five years ago."

"You must miss her a lot?"

J.D. lifted his broad shoulders in an expressive shrug.

"Yeah, I do. She was a pest when we were

growing up, always trailing around after me. Now, I only get to see her three or four times a year."

"Does she have children?"

A warm smile lit J.D.'s hard face, affection lighting the depths of his black eyes.

"Two boys, and they're little hellions! They run her ragged. But I keep telling her she deserves it because she drove me crazy when she was a kid."

Ashley watched him, fascinated by a glimpse of him totally different from the iron facade with which he faced the world.

"You like children, don't you?" she said gently, handing him a steaming mug.

He stared down into her face, her golden eyes soft as they gazed into his.

"Yeah," he said huskily. "I like kids. Do you?"

"I love children," she answered, her eyes going dreamy. "Especially babies and toddlers who you can snuggle and hug." She dropped her eyes to her cup and then lifted them. "I'd like to have six."

He nearly choked on a sip of coffee.

"Six?" He stared at her, amazement stamped on his usually stoic features.

"Yes, six," she said emphatically. "One boy and five girls."

He'd expected her to say one, or two at the most. Karla hadn't wanted any. She'd laughed derisively and told him that being pregnant would ruin her figure.

"Why five girls and only one boy?"

"Because the boy can be the oldest and protect all the girls. And it's good for a man to be raised around women. He learns to appreciate them."

"Wherever did you get such a strange idea?" he asked, fascinated.

"From the Jacobsons," she responded with a smile. "Before my parents died, we lived next to them on a farm in Iowa. Mr. Jacobson was from Norway and very blonde and blue-eyed. Mrs. Jacobson was from Iowa and she was tiny and black-haired. The children were all tow-headed, with big blue eyes, except for two little girls with dark hair." Ashley sighed, remembering. "My mother let me go to their house to play sometimes and it was so nice. They were never lonely because they always had one another to play with."

J.D. had a half-dozen important questions to ask her and couldn't decide which to ask first.

"You lived in Iowa? On a farm?" His voice was incredulous.

"Of course." she replied. "My father was a farmer just like his father before him."

"How did you wind up in New York City? I thought you grew up there."

"I did," she responded, sitting down on the sofa. She sipped the hot coffee, a reminiscent smile forming on her soft mouth. "I loved it on the farm. But," she shrugged in a way that didn't disguise the painful memories, "my parents were killed in a car crash—a drunken driver hit them head-on—and my Aunt Magda became my guardian. She was my father's sister and had been raised on the farm, but left as soon as she was eighteen. She hated life in the country and sold the farm immediately after they died. Then she took me to New York to live with her.''

J.D. seated himself beside her on the sofa, sprawling back against the pillows to watch her.

''Is she the one who got you started modeling?'' Ashley nodded.

''She owns an agency in New York. She's never been married and has no children of her own. I'm sure she had no idea at first what to do with me, but she gave me a home and took care of me. One day she had to work and didn't have a sitter to leave me with. The photographer at the shoot liked me and took some shots. Before I knew it, I was working regularly.''

''And you were only eight years old?'' He sounded indignant. Ashley glanced at him to find the black brows pulled down in a frown over dark eyes. ''Aren't there child labor laws against that kind of thing?''

Touched by his concern, Ashley covered his hand with her own where it lay against his hard thigh. Immediately, he turned his hand over and threaded his fingers through hers, his clasp firm and warm.

''It wasn't bad, J.D.,'' she reassured him, comforted by his touch. "It was probably the best thing that could have happened. I was grieving so over losing my parents that I hardly knew where I was most of the time. The work helped until time went by and I healed."

"You never stop missing them, do you?" he asked with keen perception.

Ashley sighed deeply, the old familiar tightness hurting her chest. She let out a shuddering sigh and it relieved the painful ache.

"No," she managed a small, tremulous smile. "I never stop missing them. But at least I still have my aunt." For a quiet moment, her gaze met his in sad recognition. "You miss your parents, too, don't you."

"Yeah," he said slowly, deeply. "I miss them. It gets easier, but there are times when I'm doing something that I used to do with my dad—something simple, like forking hay to the horses in the barn— and the grief hits me all over again, as if it just happened yesterday." He glanced up and met her compassionate gaze. "You know what I mean?" She nodded, her slim fingers tightening on his. "The other night," he said slowly, "when I walked into the kitchen and saw you standing at the stove cooking, I remembered running into that kitchen a hundred times when I was a kid to find my mom stirring a pan on the stove. The smells, the light, the warmth—"

"Oh, J.D.," she whispered softly, tears welling in her gold eyes. "I'm so sorry, I never thought—"

"No—don't," he hushed her softly, quick concern making him set his cup down on the table and remove hers from her unresisting fingers. It seemed perfectly natural to feel him slide his arms around her and pull her against his warm, hard body. "It was a good memory, not a bad one," he whispered softly, sifting his fingers through her hair and returning to stroke the thick silk that fell over her shoulders. For a long time they sat like that— giving and taking comfort from the other's closeness.

"Now, whenever I walk into the kitchen," he said, his slow words softly muffled against her hair, "I'll remember you standing there."

Ashley nuzzled closer in silent acceptance.

"I miss being part of a family," she murmured against his shirt. "I'd move back to that farm in Iowa in a minute if I could have a family. It's a good place to raise children. Not that I don't like New York, I do. I love the museums, the shopping, and the theater. It's just that I remember what life was like with my mother and father in the country and I want that close-to-the-land life for my children. It gives a person a solid, secure base for growing." A deep sigh lifted her breasts gently against his chest. "But given the way I feel about men, there's little chance I'll ever have children."

His lips moved in a smile against her hair.

"Not if you can't get past kissing," he said with amusement.

Ashley flushed and rapped his shoulder with one small fist in a halfhearted reprimand.

"You're making fun of me," she said grouchily.

"Never," he answered promptly, catching her fist in one big, warm hand and holding it against his chest. "And I'd never make fun of you for wanting to get married and have six kids. It's not easy being alone. I'd give anything to be able to trust someone enough to marry and have kids. The McCulloughs have been working this land since the 1800s and I'm the last of the line. If I don't have children, who will take over when I'm gone?"

Ashley tilted her head back to look up into his hard face, its usual cool remoteness replaced by pensiveness.

"Your sister has two boys. Maybe one of them will want to take over?"

J.D.'s black head moved in a negative shake.

"Maybe, but it won't be the same. They're Armstrongs, not McCulloughs."

"Uhmmm," Ashley murmured, and dropped her head back to his chest, comforted by the steady thud of his heart. "Looks like we're two of a kind, and neither of us will ever have what we really want."

Silence reigned before he spoke again. "Ashley," the words seemed torn from him, the deep voice husky. "I only need one son named McCullough to inherit all this, but I wouldn't mind having six kids."

She went perfectly still.

"You wouldn't?" she whispered, leaning away from him to look up into his intent dark face.

"No," he said softly, "I wouldn't. And a ranch is a good place to raise kids."

"Yes," she agreed in a dazed whisper. "A very good place."

"You like kissing me, don't you?"

"Oh, yes!" the words came from her mouth fervently, emphatically.

"You told me you don't mind kissing men, but you don't like anything more. And it takes a lot more than kissing to get six babies, you know that, don't you?"

She nodded, unable to speak, her gaze locked with his.

"We both go up in flames when we just kiss each other," he said slowly, "and I have a feeling it would only get hotter and better." The deep voice paused, his black eyes searching hers. "Do you really think you could give up living in the city to raise children in the country?"

"I think so."

"Would you like to—with me?"

"Are you asking me to marry you?" she asked in stunned shock—stars shining in her gold eyes—afraid to hope he really meant it.

J.D. looked down into her glowing face and

smoothed his thumb over her soft lips before pressing gently, firmly against the lush curve of her bottom lip, easing her lips apart. He bent his head until their mouths were only a whisper away.

"What would you say if I did?" he asked huskily, his warm, coffee-flavored breath puffing gently against her lips.

Ashley caught her breath, going perfectly still with hope while her gaze searched his hard face.

"Yes," she whispered in response. "I'd say yes!"

A flame leapt in the black eyes.

"Then I'm asking," he said tautly.

"I'm accepting," she said, her voice thick with emotion as she slid her arms around his neck and pulled his face to bridge that whisper's distance and bring his mouth to hers.

His big hand cradled her head while his mouth made slow, sweet love to hers. Ashley melted against him, her soft breasts resting against his chest where his heart shuddered against his ribs. Her own heart was beating wildly, the blood in her veins pulsing hotly. Without releasing her mouth, J.D. shifted until he was lying on the cushions with her soft body wrapped tightly in his arms. Her legs tangled with his, the hard muscles beneath her breathlessly exciting as she pressed closer. One of his hands moved, closing over the curve of her hip to pull her higher, closer, and she shuddered with excitement, moaning softly against his mouth.

J.D. slid his hands under her sweater, savoring the satiny texture of her skin as he stroked her back. The intense pleasure of touching her was driving him crazy. He reversed their positions until she half lay beneath him while he supported his weight with his forearms so he wouldn't crush her. She seemed so smallboned and fragile beneath his hands. He tore his mouth from hers and lifted his head to look down into her passion-dazed face. Her mouth was softly swollen from the pressure of his and he couldn't resist pressing tasting kisses against its tempting softness.

"I want to see you," he whispered, his deep voice rough with emotion. His hand slid up beneath her sweater, stroking the sides of her midriff.

"J.D., don't—" she whispered in protest, suddenly shy as she felt his hand slide lower to catch the hem of her sweater.

"Why not, honey." His eyes were heavylidded and his deep voice thicker, rougher. "Please, baby, I won't let us go too far, I promise."

She couldn't deny him and lifted her arms. He pulled the sweater over her head and tossed it aside, never taking his eyes from her. She felt a swift surge of pride as she watched the awe on his face, his cheeks flushed with arousal.

"You're beautiful." She was wearing a wisp of a bra—pink satin with cream lace. The dark rose of her nipples were visible through the lace. He nearly groaned aloud with pleasure. He lifted his gaze to her face. "I dreamed about seeing you like this," he murmured and bent to brush his lips just above the lace; his fingers stroking her in maddening circles until Ashley could bear his teasing no longer and caught his hand to press it over the thrust of one breast. His palm filled to overflowing and J.D. groaned while Ashley bit her lip to keep from crying out with pleasure.

He lifted his head to look at her face, his black hair tousled from the thrust of her fingers.

"Don't hold back, honey. Let me hear you—it lets me know you like what we're doing. You do like it, don't you?"

Ashley was barely aware when the clasp of her bra came undone and the satin slid away. She only knew that the brush of his fingers against bare skin sent heated rivers of arousal shuddering through her body. His thumb slowly stroked the peak of one breast while he watched the pleasure moving across her face.

Ashley's lids were so heavy she could barely lift them and she stared at him through a tangle of lashes, her gold eyes dark with desire.

"Yes—oh yes," she breathed. She touched his lips and he pulled a fingertip into the warm, wet hollow of his mouth, his tongue holding it while he sucked gently. "I love what we're doing. Can we—can we take your shirt off? I want to see you, too.''

J.D.'s whole body tensed, his eyes closing tightly, briefly, before they opened again to blaze hotly down at her. Slowly he withdrew her finger from his mouth, his tongue stroking one last, wet time down her palm.

"You do it," he said thickly. "Unbutton my shirt."

Ashley lifted her hands to the black buttons set in blue flannel and fumbled the first three out of their buttonholes. Beneath it, he wore a thermal undershirt with a placket opening. Already unbuttoned, it gave her access to tanned muscles and the fascinating silky curls of chest hair. Her fingers lingered over the black curls, sliding exploringly over hair-roughened skin and tugging gently, experimentally.

J.D. stood it as long as he could, nearly groaning aloud with pleasure at the feel of her hands on him, before he pulled away from her long enough to finish unbuttoning the flannel shirt, rip the shirt-tails out of his jeans, and shrug out of it. It hit the floor behind them and was quickly followed by the thermal undershirt. While he was still ripping it off over his head, Ashley's hands were sliding over the warm, muscled wall of his chest.

J.D. eased slowly down over her, his hard, hair-roughened muscles brushing against her soft bareness. Ashley gasped with pleasurable shock and slid her arms around the strong column of his neck, urging him closer. He settled gently over her, his black eyes burning hotly as he watched the erect pink nipples disappear, nestling in black hair while the swollen mounds of her breasts were crushed slowly against him.

His whole body clenched at the feel of her half-naked beneath him, her soft curves trustingly accommodating the hard line of his body. He brushed his open mouth over her face, feeling the heat build before fusing his mouth to hers.

Beneath him, Ashley was awash with uncontrolled desire, the brush of his chest against her sensitive breasts and nipples sending her nearly mindless with pleasure. His hard body gave off a furnace of heat that matched her own, fusing them from head to toe. She was burning up, her own body twisting slowly against his in response to his slow, rhythmic movements. He tore his mouth from hers and trailed openmouthed, hot kisses down her throat, moving unerringly until his lips found the sensitive peak of a breast.

Ashley jerked in reaction, her fists closing in his thick black hair as she held his head to her. She moaned his name and his lips closed over the swollen pink bud, tugging gently. She felt a river of pleasure stream from his mouth in a direct line through her body, to her abdomen, and still lower to pool heavily between her thighs. Her fingers flexed against his head and her hips bucked against his in an arch of invitation as old as Eve.

J.D. lifted his head, one hand sliding down the silky bare skin of her midriff and over the soft denim of her jeans to trace her hip and close over the back of her thigh. Ashley's hips lifted again in unconscious invitation and he bit off a groan. He lowered his gaze to look down the line of their bodies and watched her helpless, instinctive reaction as his thumb stroked slowly, repeatedly over her inner thigh. Despite that layer of denim separating her skin and his, she was beautifully responsive to his touch.

"Baby," he whispered desperately, desire painting a dark flush across his face. "Stop me! Tell me you don't want me to do this—please!" He trailed his fingers up the zipper of her jeans and slipped the single button at the waist from its buttonhole. His voice was husky, thick with emotion, as he slid his fingers beneath the waistband and spread his hand over the silky softness of her abdomen. "I thought I could control it, honey, but I can't. It's like wildfire, burning me up," he whispered, resting his forehead against hers. His thick, black lashes drifted together as he gave himself up to the wildly arousing feel of her silky skin.

Ashley was beyond helping him. The untried emotions racing through her body only urged her to submit. She twined her arms around his neck and pulled him down, her eyelids shutting as his mouth closed over hers. She gave in to the dark tides of pleasure washing in waves over her body.

Both of them were nearly beyond awareness, oblivious to the outside world. But they slowly became aware of a shrill, intrusive ringing wedging its way into their consciousness and dragging them back to reality.

"The phone," J.D. said reluctantly, unable to completely pull his mouth away from the silky skin of her face and neck.

"Uhmmm," Ashley agreed drowsily, tilting her chin to give his roving lips access to its soft, sensitive underside. "I suppose we should answer it."

"No," he grunted, willingly accepting her invitation to explore. "Let's not. Whoever it is will give up soon."

But the shrill, insistent ring continued. At last J.D. forced his hands and lips to leave the seductive addiction of her warm, silky skin. He pushed up and away from her and stood only to lean over her again, one hand resting on the bare skin of her midriff, the other tangled in her hair while he pressed one last searing kiss on her faintly swollen mouth.

"Don't go away," he whispered huskily.

"I won't," she answered. Her helpless gaze followed his lithe figure, lingering on the broad expanse of brown shoulders and the faded levis slung low on slim hips as he passed through the doorway into the kitchen.

She could hear him clearly as he picked up the receiver and growled into the phone.

"Hello."

A brief silence followed.

"Yeah, she's here, but she's kind of busy right now."

Ashley knew a brief moment of curiosity. Who could be calling her? It must be Joanne, she thought. She smoothed a hand over her midriff, still warm from J.D.'s parting caress.

"Her Aunt Magda? Sure, I'll tell her. Just a minute."

J.D.'s deep voice uttering her aunt's name hit Ashley with the force of a pail of ice water being dumped over her head. She sat upright on the sofa and grabbed up her sweater, clutching it over her bare bosom.

"Oh, my god! It's Aunt Magda!"

SEVEN

J.D. walked back through the door and halted in midstride, the width of the room between them as he stared at Ashley. She was sitting stiffly on the very edge of the sofa, her hair a tumble of silk around her bare shoulders. Her fingers clutched the red sweater over the high slope of her breasts, her gold eyes round and worried in her flushed face.

"Ashley," he said softly, treading warily across the floor to approach her with the same caution he would have used with a startled fawn. "Your aunt is on the phone. Do you want to talk to her?"

No! A voice shouted inside Ashley's brain, but she forced it down and managed a small smile of reassurance.

"Yes, of course."

J.D. cupped her chin in hard fingers and tilted her face up to his.

"Hey, honey, what is it? You don't have to talk to her if you don't want to." The deep voice was laced with concern.

"No—no, I'll talk to her."

She pulled away from him and stood. He followed her into the kitchen, his black eyes puzzled as he watched her pick up the telephone.

"Hello."

"Ashley!" Her aunt's brisk voice carried over the wire. "How are you, darling?"

"Fine, Aunt Maggie, just fine. Where are you?"

"I'm back in New York. The weather was absolutely beastly and I told Charles that if we couldn't have sunshine, I'd rather have a white Christmas in New York than a wet Christmas in Jamaica." Her breathy chuckle quickly gave Ashley a vivid picture of her aunt curled up in her favorite chair with the reciever tucked between her shoulder and ear and tiny reading glasses perched on her short, patrician nose. "But exactly where are *you*? I tried to reach you at Joanne's number and she told me Cassie was ill and you had to take a room at a neighbor's home."

"Yes—Cassie has the mumps. Maggie, do you know if I had them as a child?"

"Mmmmmh," Maggie murmured, thinking

aloud. "You had the measles and I distinctly remember you scratching with the chicken pox, but mumps? No, no, I don't think so. Of course," she added, "you could have had them before you came to stay with me."

"Yes, I suppose so," Ashley sighed, secretly relieved that her aunt couldn't remember. Much as she loved Joanne, she didn't want to leave the warm haven of J.D.'s home. Not now. Not ever.

"Well, Ashley," her aunt was saying, "that settles that. You may as well fly home since you can't spend Christmas with Joanne. If you leave tomorrow morning, you can be here in time for the little Christmas Eve get-together I'm planning. Just a spur-of-the-moment thing with a few people— fifty or so—but you'll know everyone."

Ashley suppressed a groan of dismay. She knew only too well what her aunt's "few people" meant—at least twice as many as she had planned on and shoptalk all night long.

"I don't think so, Maggie. I don't feel like traveling. I'll just stick with my original plan and spend Christmas here and fly home before New Year's Eve."

"But, Ashley," Maggie sounded confused, "you don't really want to spend Christmas with some strange family, do you?"

"J.D.'s not strange," Ashley answered calmly. "I've grown to know him quite well over the last few days and I really do want to spend Christmas here.''

''J.D.?'' Maggie's voice reflected even more confusion and a hint of worry. ''Is he married? Joanne didn't actually say you were staying with a married man, but she led me to believe you were with a family.''

Warm lips brushed her bare shoulder and Ashley jumped, swinging her head quickly to find J.D. close behind her, his black hair brushing her neck while he bent to her.

She suppressed a gasp and struggled to keep her voice calm and level.

''No, no, he's not married.''

''Are you sure you should be staying with him? I mean, what do you know about this person?'' Maggie's voice was now definitely alarmed.

''I'm sure it's perfectly all right, Maggie, and Joanne has known him all her life.'' Ashley tried to sound reassuring, but it was difficult when all she wanted to do was drop the receiver and melt into J.D.'s arms as he slid them around her waist and pulled her against him.

''Sometimes men you've known all your life turn out to be Jack the Ripper!''

''I'm sure he won't turn into Jack the Ripper.'' Ashley managed to say with confidence, a shiver rippling over her as J.D. grinned and nipped her shoulder threateningly. ''You worry too much,

Maggie. I'm perfectly safe. I really must run. Tell Charlie hello and Merry Christmas to the both of you. I'll see you before New Year's."

"Very well," Maggie sounded unconvinced and her good-bye was reluctant.

Ashley managed to replace the receiver and turned in the circle of J.D.'s arms. But just when she would have pulled him close, he held her off with his hands at her waist.

"Is everything all right?"

"Fine, just fine." She managed a small smile.

"Hey, you're going to have to learn not to lie to me, not even little fibs," he chided gently. "When I walked into the living room to tell you your aunt was on the phone, you looked like a deer on the first day of hunting season."

She started to protest, but it died a quick death at the warm concern in his black eyes. She sighed and gave in.

"It was just such a shock after—after we—" She blushed and looked down to avoid his gaze.

His palm smoothed over the silky crown of her head and he urged her gently closer until her forehead rested against his chest, his other arm slid around her waist to hug her against him.

"Kind of like having her walk in on us making love?" he asked gently, his deep voice rumbling beneath her ear.

She nodded, her cheek rubbing against the warmth of his skin and muscle.

"I'm sorry, honey. But you know, it's probably a good thing she called when she did," he said reflectively.

"Why?" Ashley was bewildered. She knew she was having second thoughts, but why was he?

"Because," he leaned his head back to look down into her flushed face, "I think we should be married before we start making babies, don't you?"

Ashley nodded, suddenly shy and abruptly aware that the sweater was no longer clutched against her and her bare torso was pressed intimately against his.

"Most men don't care about that," she said, looking up curiously at him as a sudden thought hit her. "Do you—did you ever have other children?"

His arms turned into bands of steel, his body grew taut, and the black eyes blazed with bitter pain.

"I don't know for sure," he said harshly, his face once again a cold, hard mask. He stared at her as if he didn't really see her. "A friend told me that Karla got rid of my baby after I went to 'Nam, but she never admitted it so I'll never know."

"I'm so sorry, J.D." Ashley stroked his cheek with gentle, soothing motions, as a quick fury at the woman who had hurt him flared inside her.

"That's something you should know about me," he said, fixing her with a hot, fierce stare. "I know it's an old-fashioned idea, but I believe children are gifts from God, not inconvenient accidents that clutter up their parents' lives.''

Quick tears stood in Ashley's gold eyes and spangled her long lashes.

''I agree,'' she said quietly, her gaze fixed on his as she felt the tension leave his hard body and the fierce intensity fade from his black stare.

His chest lifted in a heavy sigh and he folded her close again, as her arms went around him naturally.

''It's not that I think wives should be kept barefoot and pregnant,'' he said quietly against her hair. ''I'm not that much of a male chauvinist. I'll take precautions to protect you until you're ready to have children. It's just that if God gives us a baby, I don't want you to flush it away.''

''I understand. I feel the same way.'' She tilted her head back to look up at him, her hair spilling in a silken waterfall down over his hands. He bent his head and kissed her. It was a vow, a promise, a sealing of two hearts in perfect accord. When he lifted his mouth from hers, they were both shaken.

J.D. released her and bent to pick up the red sweater from where it had dropped unnoticed to the linoleum.

''If we don't get you covered,'' he said unsteadily, ''I'm not going to be able to keep my hands off you.''

He pulled the sweater over her head and she

lifted her arms like an obedient child to slip into
it.

"There," he said gruffly, his big hands tugging
her hair free from the red wool and smoothing it
over her shoulders. His black gaze drifted down
her throat and over the thrust of her unbound
breasts beneath the sweater and he nearly groaned
aloud. Even covered with the loose sweater, she
still tempted him almost beyond bearing. Reso-
lutely, he reined in his rioting senses. "If we don't
get started on your tree, it won't be decorated in
time for Christmas."

Ashley smiled and slipped her hand into his. He
looked faintly shocked for a moment before his
fingers contracted, catching hers in a warm, close
clasp. He smiled, flashing those dimples beside his
lips that Ashley had grown to love. Contented,
they strolled into the living room.

Ashley bent toward the dresser mirror, humming with the radio as it played "White Christmas" while she fastened silver hoops in her earlobes.
Finished, she stepped back and ran a critical eye
over her reflection. The red velvet dress she'd
bought especially for Christmas fell to midcalf. It
had a formfitting bodice with a draped neckline,
tight waist, and tiny cap sleeves. The lines were
classic and deceptively modest, but the dress hugged
her curves faithfully. She sprayed her favorite per-

fume behind her ears and knees and along the velvet neckline.

J.D. was taking her to Christmas Eve church services. It was the first time she had had the opportunity to dress up for him and she wondered nervously if he would like her dress. She fidgeted with her hair. *Would it be better twisted up?* She pulled it high, away from her face.

No. She let it fall to her shoulders and ran a brush through it to smooth out the tangles. *Loose is better.*

She took a deep breath and pressed a hand against her midriff where her stomach was churning.

This is silly, she said sternly to the woman in the mirror. *You know he doesn't think you're ugly.*

But I want him to think I'm perfect, an inner voice wailed.

Balderdash, her other self scoffed. *What you want is for the man to take one look at you and want to tear your clothes off.*

Ashley grew serious and continued to stare at the solemn, golden-eyed woman in the mirror.

Yes, I really do, she thought with stark honesty. *I wonder if that makes me a loose woman? No,* she answered herself. *I've never felt this way about anyone else. Only J.D. And I love him. And he loves me, too, even if he doesn't know it yet.*

"But he will," she muttered aloud, tilting her chin challengingly, a stubborn, determined gleam in her eye. "He thinks all he wants from me is

sons to help him work this ranch and inherit it
someday, but he's going to get more than he bar-
gained for." Her eyes narrowed and a small, se-
cret smile tilted her lush mouth. "Starting tonight!
I'm going to give him a Christmas present he'll
never forget!"

Knuckles rapped against the door, startling her
from her thoughts.

"Ashley, honey," the deep male voice carried
easily through the bedroom door. "Are you ready?"

"Yes—come in," she turned to pick up the fur
coat from the bed. When she turned back, he was
standing in the door staring at her. She stared
back. He was gorgeous. The collar of a white
dress shirt was just visible beneath a white cable-
knit sweater; his skin tan against the creamy white.
Black wool slacks hugged muscled thighs and tight
buttocks as perfectly as the worn denim Ashley
was used to seeing him wear. Gleaming black
cowboy boots covered his feet. She sighed unconsciously and smiled dreamily at him. "You're
beautiful!"

Red color flushed along the hard thrust of his
cheekbones.

"That's supposed to be my line," he said, his
voice rasping above a throat gone dry from looking at her. She was wearing a red dress of some
sort of soft material that clung to every curve and line
of her body. Silver hoops swung from her ears,

glinting in the fall of sable hair that brushed her shoulders. The dress was ladylike and proper, but all J.D. could think about was unzipping it and taking it off the soft body it covered. It was all he could do to keep from crossing the room and doing just that. "We, uhmm," he swallowed and tried again. "We better be going if we want to find seats. The church fills up early on Christmas Eve."

"Okay." Ashley smiled at him demurely, concealing her satisfaction at his reaction. She held out the fur coat and he strode quickly to her and held it while she slipped into it. His hands lingered on her shoulders and he dropped his face for one brief moment to rest against the perfumed fragrance of silky hair before pulling away.

"Let's get out of this damn bedroom," he growled, his patience strained. "Or we're never going to make it out of the house tonight."

Ashley widened her eyes and looked at him.

"Why, J.D., whatever do you mean? I thought you said you didn't want to practice making babies until after we're married?"

"Stop that," he swatted her backside but she barely felt it through the heavy coat. "I've warned you enough times about teasing me!"

Ashley laughed happily and they left the room.

The service was beautiful. Afterward, as they made their way slowly down the aisle and into the vestibule, Ashley was vividly aware of the curious glances sent their way. Some of them were covert, others were openly, unabashedly quizzical.

"J.D.," she whispered, her arm threaded through the crook of his. He bent his black head and she reached up to him, her lips brushing against his ear. "Why are people staring at us? Is there something wrong with me? "

J.D. glanced around them, nodding to several of his neighbors, before looking back down into her upturned face.

"It's not you, honey, it's me."

Confusion flickered across her expressive features.

"You? I don't understand."

"They're not used to seeing me with a woman, especially one as beautiful as you."

"Oh." She thought about that for a moment before asking, "Does that mean that you don't date often, or that you only date not-beautiful women?"

His eyes narrowed at her innocent look; his mouth quirked in a half grin.

"That means I don't date. Period. Not beautiful women and not not-beautiful women."

"Oh." Her features settled into a pleased look.

Before J.D. could say anything else, they were standing in front of the minister shaking his hand and murmuring their appreciation. They stepped out into the cold air and hurried across the snowy parking lot to J.D.'s truck.

"Brrrrr! This reminds me of the night you took

me to Joanne's from the Blue Cougar. It's freezing in here!'' She snuggled into the coat, pushing her gloved hands up into the sleeves to hug herself for warmth.

"It'll be warm in a minute," he turned to look at her, remembering that drive from the bar and his curiosity about what she looked like beneath the concealing fur coat. Now he knew, and the desire he felt that first night was stronger. It was mixed with a curious longing that became a sweet ache when she smiled at him, her gold eyes turning warm and liquid. But he refused to put a name to the emotion that surged through him. They were physically compatible, they both wanted marriage and a family, and he would be a good provider.

When they were at last on the highway with the snowy moonlit landscape sliding by outside, J.D. glanced across at her.

"What are you doing way over there? Come here."

He lifted his arm and she slid nearer to be tucked close against his side. His fingers toyed with her hair and stroked the soft skin of her cheek. Ashley nuzzled against him and smiled with contentment.

The big truck slid on a patch of ice and she gasped, her hand instinctively steadying her against the nearest solid object, which in this case happened to be J.D.'s thigh. The hard muscles flexed beneath her fingers and for a few nervous moments he needed both hands on the steering wheel before the big tires found traction again.

"You okay?" He glanced down at her, his black gaze noting the apprehension in her gold eyes.

"Fine," she said shakily. "I'm glad you're driving and not me."

He smiled and concentrated on the road. The temperature had dropped and frozen patches of ice made driving treacherous, but the night was beautiful—a perfect Christmas Eve with clear moonlight sparkling on the snow and stars glittering in the black dome of the sky.

Heat spread from Ashley's hand on his thigh to pool heavily in his groin. He covered her gloved fingers with his own. J.D. toyed with his need to push her hand six inches higher before he conquered the urge. He was so hot he was ready to explode, but he was determined to let her go to her marriage bed untouched. Just how the hell he was going to manage that, he had no idea.

The house was welcomingly warm. When J.D. closed the heavy front door behind them and flicked the switch, the living room lamps came on and so did the tree lights. The embers of a fire still glowed on the hearth. J.D. knelt on the stone hearth and stirred the glowing coals; the flames quickly grew and licked greedily at the dry wood.

"Would you like something to drink?" she asked.

He glanced over his shoulder to find Ashley standing behind him.

"Sure. I think there's wine in the kitchen."

"I'll get it."

The dress slithered against her legs as she moved. J.D. watched her hungrily as she left the room, her hips swaying gently beneath the red velvet.

He wanted her so badly his teeth ached, and other parts of his body he didn't want to think about were screaming at him. He could easily seduce her. Every time she looked at him with those dreamy gold eyes he was reminded that she was willing. But one of them had to be sensible. He'd be damned if he'd chance getting her pregnant before they were married. And he refused to admit, even to himself, that an instinctive, gut feeling warned him that once he'd had her, she would have a hold on him that no one else had ever had.

We'll have a glass of wine, a little conversation, then go to bed—alone.

Satisfied that he could handle the situation, he stood and pulled off the creamy sweater. Before he dropped onto the sofa, he had second thoughts and sank into the big leather recliner. *Safer to have her across the room on the sofa,* he decided. *Where I can look, but not touch.*

Ashley came through the door from the kitchen, a glass of wine in each hand. Her steps barely faltered when she saw him stretched out in the big recliner, a small smile tilting her mouth. *So that's your plan,* she thought with amusement. *Sorry, big man, but it's not going to work.*

She swayed slowly across the room, knowing his gaze was riveted on her.

"Here's your wine," she offered, her fingers lingering on his when he took the glass. She perched, facing him, on the arm of the recliner and sipped her wine, watching him over the rim of her glass. The cuffs of his shirt were folded up over his forearms. She ran a slow finger down the exposed brown skin to trace the bones of his wrist and down the hair-dusted back of his strong hand. "The services were lovely tonight," she said absently, entranced by the warm skin beneath her fingertips.

"Yeah," he said hoarsely, his black gaze sliding intently over the lovely line of her throat and shoulders. He couldn't have told her a word the minister said. He'd been too busy stealing looks at her profile; too entranced as her clear soprano sang the well-loved carols.

"Do you suppose your friends will get used to seeing us together?" she asked softly, shifting her attention to the unfastened buttons at his neck where brown skin and black curls beckoned enticingly. She toyed absently with the line of buttons until her fingers could smooth over his chest inside the opened shirt collar.

He started to answer and found his voice wouldn't work. He tried again.

"Sure they will," the deep voice rasped from his dry throat.

She leaned toward him, her hand fumbling her wineglass onto the magazine table beside the chair.

Her perfume wafted toward him and he drew in a deep breath. Her thick black lashes were half-lowered over those gold eyes; her darkened gaze focused on his body was arousing as hell.

He wasn't sure exactly how it happened, but somehow she slid off the chair arm and into his lap. He set his wineglass down on the floor. His fingers seemed to have a mind of their own as they slid up the silky curve of her calf.

"We shouldn't be doing this," he growled throatily, dropping his face to bury it in her hair and draw in a deep breath, which flooded him with the scent that was uniquely hers.

"Why not?" she murmured drowsily, her fingers twisting two more buttons free so she could nuzzle against his hair-roughened skin. "Uhmmm, you smell so good." Everything female in her responded to him, making her bones go fluid, curving her closer in his arms.

"God, Ashley," he groaned, squeezing his eyes shut in a vain attempt to shut out the spell she was weaving. "Don't do this! We have to stop!"

"Why?" She opened her mouth and flicked her tongue experimentally against his skin. He tasted faintly salty, mixed with soap. "You taste good, too," she murmured distractedly.

J.D.'s big body jerked in reaction. One hand cupped the back of her head and moved it slowly from side to side, brushing her open mouth back and forth over his skin. His heart shuddered beneath her mouth, his skin hot beneath her tongue.

"Do you like that?" she whispered, tilting her head to look at him. His black eyes were hot, a flush of red streaked his cheeks with arousal.

"Yeah," he muttered hoarsely. "I like it."

He bent his head and took her mouth in a hot, wet kiss. She lost track of time. The hard body she lay against, coupled with the seductive lure of his mouth, hazed her senses, narrowing the world to only the two of them. She curled her body unconsciously into his, her legs shifting to send the velvet skirt sliding up her thigh. J.D.'s hand followed, his fingers moving in a rhythmic caress over the soft, sensitive backs of her knees before sliding higher until they reached the bare skin above the tops of her stockings. His body tensed and he lifted his head to look down at her.

His deeply tanned hand was even darker against the paleness of her thigh. His thumb smoothed again and again over skin and silk and lace.

"The first night you stayed here," he whispered huskily, "when I put you to bed, your dress slid up and you were wearing garters. Are these the same ones?"

"Yes," she confessed, finding it incredibly erotic to watch the movements of his darker skin against hers.

"I've had dreams about you and those lacy little

things every night since then,'' he said in a bla-
tantly sensuous tone. His heavy-lidded gaze lifted
from her legs to her face, and back down her
throat and the rapid rise and fall of her breasts
beneath the red velvet. ''Are you wearing anything
else under that dress?''

''No, not much,'' she breathed, watching his
eyes dilate at her response.

The last of J.D.'s noble intentions melted like
ice under a blowtorch. She was clearly willing and
he was damn sure ready! To hell with it, he'd take
her tonight and marry her tomorrow. He was beyond
being reasonable.

EIGHT

Ashley knew the moment he made up his mind. She read the implacable male intent in his hot black stare as clearly as if he'd shouted the words. She made no protest when he slid his arms under her and surged out of the chair. She tucked her face beneath his chin as he strode quickly across the room and up the stairs and down the hall to his bedroom. He didn't bother to turn on the lamps, but the moonlight streaming through the windows gave the room a silvery light.

He released her legs and shuddered with pleasure as they slid slowly down his body until she stood before him. His mouth claimed hers again as if he couldn't bear to be separated from her. His arms went around her, his fingers unhooking the top of her dress and he slid the zipper down past her waist. Still holding her mouth with his, he arched away from her and pushed the dress down her arms and over her hips to let it fall in a dark pool at her feet. He lifted his head from hers and looked down at her, his chest tight in a harsh indrawn breath.

She wore only a brief bra of white silk and lace with matching bikini panties and those frilly garters. The moonlight brushed her with silver, shadowing her eyes and gleaming off her cheeks and lips, the delicate bones of smooth shoulders, and the inward sweep of waist, the outward swell of thighs. He reached out and drew her slowly to him, his hands trembling with the effort to keep from crushing her against him. His eyes blazed black fire and she stretched her arms up to circle his neck. The movement caused her breasts to swell against the restraining silk and he bent his head to brush hot kisses across the bare skin. Calloused fingers moved against her back and the brief silk and lace bra fell away, giving his lips freer access to the soft slope of her breasts. Ashley shuddered and held him to her, nearly mindless with the faintly abrasive brush of wool slacks and cotton shirt against her sensitized skin.

"Please," she whispered, her voice thick with need as she slid her hands down his arms to tug at the material that kept his skin from hers.

"What do you want, baby," he breathed, his

lips moving against the soft skin of her throat. "Tell me."

"Off," she managed to get out. "Take your shirt off."

She fumbled with the buttons and he helped her, shrugging out of the shirt without losing contact with her. She gasped with pleasure when he was bare and she could feel the warmth of his skin against hers. The hair that arrowed down his chest was pleasantly rough. She twisted slowly, brushing her body against his.

J.D. groaned and reluctantly pulled away from her to yank the blue comforter and matching sheets down the bed. With an economy of movement, he picked her up and settled her against the sheets before dropping onto the edge of the bed to tug off his boots. They hit the floor with haphazard thuds before he stood to unzip his slacks and step out of them. He barely had enough control to remember not to strip off his briefs. If someone as beautiful and desirable as Ashley was a virgin, he didn't want to shock her. He needed to take his time with her. He'd always heard that a woman's first time was painful and maybe even frightening. He only hoped he was capable of controlling himself long enough not to hurt her.

He slid into the bed and her waiting arms, the feel of her silky, warm body stretched half beneath his sending him crazy with excitement. He sealed his mouth over hers and tried to force himself to slow down.

Ashley had no idea of the thoughts going through his mind. She was incapable of anything other than the elemental urge to mate. His long legs tangled with hers, muscled and hair-roughened against her smooth softness. When his hand slid over her thigh and traced the lacy line of her high French-cut bikini up her bottom and trailed back down her abdomen she was beyond protesting. She could only moan and twist toward his hand as he slipped his fingers beneath the white lace to stroke her. She was burning up with need, moaning feverishly beneath his mouth. She barely knew it when he unsnapped the garters and slid them and the panties down her legs. It wasn't until he settled heavily between her thighs and she felt the first gentle probing that she tensed.

He lifted his head to look down at her.

"I won't hurt you if I can help it, baby," he whispered soothingly, stroking her wildly tousled hair back from her cheek. "I've heard the first time always hurts a little, but afterward I'll make it good for you. I promise."

Reassured, the faintly wary look left her eyes and they started to drift closed again.

"No," he said huskily. "Open your eyes. Watch me—then I'll know if it hurts and if I should stop."

"I don't want you to stop," she whispered feverishly, her nails scoring the hard muscles of his back. "Please—"

"I won't, honey," he soothed. "Just don't close your eyes."

So she kept them open and gold stared into black while he entered her slowly, carefully. He felt and saw the momentary pain as he breached the fragile barrier. She saw the waves of pleasure wash over his hard face as he felt her close around him like a velvet fist.

He tried to take it slow, to give her enough time, but she wound her arms around him, twisting and moaning in his arms, and it was all he could do to hold out until he felt her shudder with the ultimate pleasure before he gave in to the hot, black tide of passion that swept him into near unconsciousness.

When he roused, it was to find her still locked in his arms, their bodies pressed tightly, damply together. He lifted his head to look down at her.

"Are you all right?" his voice rasped. Her face glowed and her hair was a dark tangle across her pillow. The lush line of her lips was bare and faintly swollen from the long pressure of his.

"I'm wonderful," she smiled, stretching beneath him with feline satisfaction.

"You sure are," he teased softly. "I don't think we have to worry about your liking more than kissing, do you?" She flushed and he laughed softly and bent to taste her mouth again. When he lifted his head, she protested.

"Don't stop."

"I have to," he growled. "If I don't, we're going to do this all over again and it's too soon for you."

"Why?" she asked with naive curiosity. "Can't women do it more than once a night?"

"You sure are innocent for a city woman," he chuckled and hugged her against him. "For your information, yes, women can do 'it' more than once a night. But it was your first time and I don't want to keep at you until you're so sore you can't walk. Did I hurt you?"

"No," Ashley's eyes darkened with remembered hunger. "No," she said softly, "it was wonderful. I wish I'd met you a long time ago. What a lot of time I've wasted! Is it always like that?"

J.D.'s chest squeezed tightly.

"I don't know, honey," he answered truthfully. "It's never been like that before for me." And it hadn't. He'd had sex with other women and it always felt good, but he'd never made love before, not like this. He felt more than satisfied. He felt complete. He pushed away deeper questions about why it was different with Ashley.

He eased off her and tugged the covers up before settling her against his side, her head resting on his arm, her fingers splayed across his chest.

"Go to sleep, sweetheart, tomorrow is Christmas."

"Mmmmh," she mumbled sleepily. "It's after midnight, so it's already Christmas. Did you like your present?"

Startled, J.D. tilted his head to look down at her, but she was already asleep, burrowing against him.

"Yeah," he whispered against the thick cloud of hair. "I loved my present."

Unused to sleeping with anyone, Ashley awoke several times during the night only to sigh with contentment and snuggle closer as she realized that the hard male body she lay curled against was J.D.'s. Each time, he stirred too, murmuring soothingly until she was settled again. She woke at dawn to find his hand moving over her breasts and down to her belly and then smoothing back up to her throat and shoulders. The rhythmic stroking aroused her before she was even fully awake. Her eyes unopened, she reached for him, whispering incoherent words of love and need. Just as the sun burst over the horizon and filtered weak winter light into the room, they came together with a heat that rivaled the fiery orb. Sated, they fell asleep again in a tangle of arms, legs, and damp bodies.

"Good morning, sleepyhead."

The lazy drawl penetrated the warm cocoon of sleep that cushioned Ashley. She sighed, stretching langorously beneath sheets that felt sensuous against her bare skin. The scent of fresh-brewed coffee tickled her nostrils and she slitted her eyes open to see J.D. watching the movements of her body under the covers with frank male appreciation.

He held two steaming mugs of coffee and Ashley sat up, tucking the covers under her arms and pushing the pillows against the headboard. She leaned back against the soft cushion and smiled up at him.

"Hi," she breathed softly, a wealth of meaning in the single word. She had no idea what one said to one's lover the morning after. Her face flushed with delicate color under his warm, black stare.

"Hi," he answered, just as softly. He handed her one of the mugs and sat on the edge of the bed, his thigh pressed against hers. He slid a hand under her hair. Then he bent and took her mouth with his in a slow, savoring kiss, that treasured her lips.

When he lifted his black head to look at her, she was breathing quickly, her heart thudding against her ribs.

"I thought you were going to sleep the day away," he teased huskily.

Ashley sipped her coffee and watched him through lowered lashes.

Dear God, he looked good in the morning! His black hair was still damp from his shower and he smelled like soap and shaving cream. Faded levis clung to his thighs and he'd rolled up the cuffs of a long-sleeved blue cotton shirt to his elbows. She wasn't sure why, but the sight of his hair-dusted forearms made her weak in the knees.

"What time is it?" she asked absentmindedly, trying to concentrate on something other than the memories of all the things they'd done last night.

"Only ten-thirty," he said, sipping his coffee while his black eyes took a leisurely inventory of her ruffled hair, flushed cheeks, and bare shoulders.

"Oh." She answered distractedly, watching the black eyes darken as his gaze fixed on the tops of her breasts above the concealing sheet. Suddenly, his words sank in and she jumped, nearly spilling the coffee. "Ten-thirty! Oh, my goodness!"

"Hey, what's the matter?" J.D. held his mug out over the floor as she struggled to get off the bed without losing the sheet. The bed dipped and rocked.

"It's ten-thirty! If I don't get the turkey in the oven by eleven, it'll never get done in time!"

"Dinner?" he stared at her in dumbfounded surprise. "All this excitement is over dinner?"

She shot him a fuming glance and tugged on the blanket.

"I've planned a great Christmas dinner and if I don't hurry up, my schedule will be impossible!" She tugged on the blanket again. "Get up! You're sitting on my blanket!"

Realization dawned on him and he grinned at her—a slow, male tilting of lips that told her he enjoyed her predicament.

"Nope, you're wrong. This is my bed and my blanket."

"Please, J.D., move!" she pleaded. "I have to take a shower and get downstairs."

"Go ahead, honey, the shower's right down the hall. You don't need a blanket to get there, it's not cold at all."

She glared at his smiling face and leaned over to set the half-empty coffee mug on the bedside table. When she bent over, she spied his white shirt lying on the floor. She swiftly snagged it and dragged it into the bed with her.

"That," he argued amiably with a quirk of black brows, "is dirty pool, darlin'. And just when I was looking forward to seeing what you've been hiding under my blanket."

Ashley shrugged into the shirt and twisted and turned to get it buttoned beneath the sheets. She slid her legs out of the bed and stood, tossing the blanket back to half cover J.D. He laughed and lay sprawled across the bed, appreciating the view of her long legs under the hem of his shirt as she flounced out of the room.

Dinner was a rousing success, even though J.D. kept interrupting Ashley as she worked in the kitchen—sliding his hands around her from behind to fondle, tease, and touch. He wouldn't leave her alone and she finally set him to work chopping vegetables at the table. The moment she put the last pumpkin pie into the oven, he swung her up into his arms and carried her back upstairs to tumble her onto his rumpled bed. After dinner, they sat wrapped in each others arms on the sofa and watched *Casablanca*. When Ashley cried at the end, he mopped up her tears with his handkerchief and carried her back upstairs to his room.

"You make a wonderful Rhett Butler," she said dreamily, pressing damp kisses against his neck just below his ear. "Are you always going to carry me upstairs?"

"Whatever it takes to get you into my bed, darlin'," he drawled, "I'll do."

"All you have to do is ask," she whispered.

His arms contracted and he bent his mouth to hers, shouldering through the doorway to his room and falling onto the bed without letting go of her. Dark magic spun them into a world of sighs and groans of heated pleasure.

Ashley was cooking breakfast in the homey kitchen, humming along with Elton John on the radio, when J.D. came downstairs the next morning. He prowled barefooted and bare chested across the linoleum and took her in his arms from behind, burying his face in the sweet, warm curve of her neck and shoulder.

"Good morning," he growled, inhaling the perfumed scent of her skin and hair.

"Good morning," Ashley answered softly, tipping her head to give him access to the sensitive skin below her ear. "Uhmmm," her senses reeled. The popping sound of the bacon cooking in the pan pulled her back to awareness. "Stop that, the bacon's going to burn!"

"Who cares?" he drawled huskily, reaching around her to turn off the burner. "What are you doing out of bed this early? I don't like waking up and not having you beside me."

"It's not early. It's after ten o'clock," Ashley protested, turning in his arms to face him. A night's growth of beard shadowed his jaw, his chest was bare above the worn Levis slung low on his hips. She lifted her hands and rested them against his chest, fingers compulsively smoothing over warm, sleek skin.

His hands slid down her back and cupped her bottom, pulling her up and into the cradle of his hard thighs.

"It's too early, come back to bed," he muttered unsteadily against her mouth before his lips parted to take hers.

Her arms wound around his neck, her fingers spearing through his silky black hair, her eyes drifting closed as his mouth seduced her. J.D. felt her surrender and lifted her off the floor and started toward the door, his mouth still locked to hers.

Insistent knocking slowly pierced the haze of arousal that held them. J.D. reluctantly took his lips from Ashley's.

"Somebody's at the door," he growled with irritation.

"I suppose we should answer it," Ashley said, her lips brushing his as she spoke.

He bit off a curse and lowered her, his black eyes going hot as the notch of her thighs slid down his. He pressed a quick, searing kiss against her mouth.

"I'll get rid of whoever it is," he promised and strode out of the room.

Ashley heard the front door open and the murmur of voices. J.D.'s deep bass was interspersed with softer tones. Curious, she took a step toward the kitchen door, but stopped as J.D. pushed it open and stepped into the room. His black gaze was remote as it focused on Ashley. The woman who stepped into the room behind him was dressed in a fur-trimmed black coat and hat and exuded city chic.

Ashley's mouth dropped open.

NINE

"Aunt Maggie!" she squealed in surprise. "What are you doing here?"

Magda Tierney's green eyes flickered over the bare expanse of the broad chest and barefeet of the black-haired man who eyed her with emotionless black eyes before she appraised her niece's tousled hair, pink face, and the bare lips that gave every appearance of having just been thoroughly kissed.

"I was worried about you," she said dryly. Her gaze returned to J.D. "It appears I had good cause."

J.D. tensed, arms dropping from where they had been folded across his chest.

Ashley took one look at him and hurried into speech.

"You didn't need to worry, Maggie." She stepped quickly over to J.D. to slip her hand into his. "This is my Aunt Maggie, J.D. Maggie, this is J.D. McCullough—we're getting married!"

Magda couldn't have been more shocked if Ashley had told her she was flying to the moon.

"You're what?" she said slowly, staring at Ashley as if she'd lost her mind.

"We're getting married," Ashley positively glowed. "Isn't it wonderful?"

J.D. looked down at her love-softened face and his hard face grew gentle, the black eyes that had been perfectly cold only a moment before now warmed with fire.

"Oh, my God," Maggie said with heartfelt weariness. "It's worse than I thought."

J. D's gaze hardened again as it swept over the chic blonde woman facing them, his fingers closed protectively, possessively over Ashley's.

"Just what do you mean by that?" The deep voice was chilly with an underlying, controlled anger that was menacing.

"The obvious, of course," Maggie replied. "I have nothing against you, young man, but surely even you can see that marriage between the two of you is completely impossible."

Ashley's fingers chilled as they clung for support to J.D.'s.

"Aunt Maggie," she protested. "You don't understand—"

"Of course I do, darling," Magda interrupted. She lifted a hand toward J.D. "He's very handsome and you're very lonely. Why do you think I've been parading every eligible bachelor in Manhattan in front of you for the last eight months? I know you want a home of your own and a family. But you can't marry an Idaho rancher!"

"What's wrong with being an Idaho rancher?" J.D. ground out through set teeth, struggling to keep his temper and be polite to this woman who meant so much to Ashley.

"Nothing, absolutely nothing—if you're planning to marry an Idaho woman. But if you want to marry a model who works in New York City, it's absolutely impossible. Where will you live? Here? If you do, she'll be gone for at least nine out of every twelve months. Or will you move to New York? Can you give up mountains and fresh air for concrete and skyscrapers and a wife who works twelve to fifteen hour days and flys out of the country every few months?"

"We've already discussed that, Maggie," Ashley replied, her clear voice determined. "I'm giving up modeling. I'll go back to New York to pack my things, but then I'm coming back here to live."

Ashley's aunt stared at her in shocked horror.

"You can't mean to give up your career. You're at the very top of your profession. There isn't a woman in America who wouldn't trade places with you. You have everything any woman could ever want.''

"That's exactly it, Maggie," Ashley said earnestly, her fingers gripping J.D.'s tightly. "I don't have everything I want. I want more than a career; I want time for a husband and a family and I want that husband to be J.D.''

"You can't have thought this through," Maggie said, shaking her blonde head slowly. "To give up modeling after all your years of hard work—"

"I've been thinking of changing careers for a long time, Maggie," Ashley said quietly. "I know it's what you want for me, but for quite some time now I've been working at sketching. Before I left New York, John Adams, the art director, called me about doing some illustrating for a children's book by one of my favorite authors.''

"You didn't mention it to me." Maggie stared at her, hurt.

"I was going to as soon as this vacation was over. I needed this time away from New York to think about it.''

Maggie passed a weary hand over her brow.

"Well, in any event, you'll have plenty of time to decide if this is really what you want.''

"What do you mean?" J.D. asked with a sense of foreboding.

Maggie's green gaze met his piercing black stare without flinching.

"Ashley has contractual obligations that will

tie her up for the next four months. That should be plenty of time for her to decide if this is just a passing fancy or the real thing."

"Cancel them!" he ordered, his fingers crushing Ashley's in an unconsciously punishing grip.

"I can't." Maggie shook her head stubbornly in a movement reminiscent of Ashley. It was easy to see this woman was Ashley's aunt. "The contracts were signed months ago."

"I don't care. Get someone else. Cancel them." J.D. was implacable.

"J.D.," Ashley said softly, nearly sick with the realization that Magda was right. The life she had left a week ago, with all its obligations and responsibilities, was intruding with harsh reality on the lovely dreamworld that held only J.D. and herself. She slid her free hand up his bare arm to get his attention. He turned his black head to look down at her. "I hate to admit it, but I'm afraid she's right. I can't just walk out on my contracts."

The bicep beneath her fingers bunched, his big body going taut with tension. Black eyes turned bleak.

"Are you telling me you'd leave me and go back to New York for four months?" he asked tensely, his gaze probing hers.

"I think I'll have to, but the time will pass, J.D., and when I come back we can—"

"No," he said, releasing her hand and giving her a look that smacked of cool revulsion. "I don't think so. If you leave now, you won't be back. And I won't want you back.''

Ashley stared up into his hard face with bewildered shock. His face was the face of the bitter desperado in the Blue Cougar.

"J.D., you don't mean that,'' she said softly, pleadingly. "You can't ask me to walk out on my contracts. I gave my word. It's not something you would ever do. It's not something I would ever ask you to do.''

"I'm asking you to choose, Ashley. Me or the city and modeling.''

Tears welled in her golden eyes.

"You're not being fair! It's not that easy!''

"It is to me,'' he said. He watched the tears well and spill over to slide silently down her face. He felt like he was bleeding from a thousand deep wounds, pain racked his body, rejection screamed along stretched nerves. "I'm not like Joanne. I won't settle for a friend who jets in and out of my life every couple of years.''

"J.D., it won't be like that! Please—'' She reached to touch him, but he shrugged off her hand.

"No. You either stay now or go for good.''

"J.D., I can't—''

"That's it then.'' He interrupted her, one hand slicing the air with decision. "Call me when you're packed. I'll carry your bags down.''

And with that, he turned and left the room,

leaving Ashley desolate, hot tears streaming down her white face.

Maggie had never seen her in such pain, the golden eyes blind with it as she turned to look at her aunt.

"Maggie, I can't lose him."

"Hush," she soothed and slid a consoling arm around the slender, shaking shoulders. "It'll be all right, you'll see."

But by the time Maggie managed to pack Ashley's bags, she wasn't at all sure Ashley was going to be all right. The last time she'd seen those beloved golden eyes stricken with such a depth of pain was when she'd taken the eight-year-old girl home after the death of her parents.

She put the bags in the hallway and went downstairs to ask a stone-faced J.D. to carry them to her car. He didn't say a word, but he brushed past her and moments later descended with the suitcases and took them outside. The slamming of car doors told her that he'd put them in the rented sedan.

"Ashley!" she called up the stairwell. "Ashley, come down, dear. It's time to leave."

Just as she thought she would have to go and coax her down, Ashley appeared at the top of the stairs wearing her fur coat over jeans and a sweater. On anyone else it would have looked ridiculous, but on Ashley even jeans and Reeboks looked elegant with mink. She was halfway down the stairs when J.D. pushed open the door and stepped inside.

They both halted, her anguished golden gaze meeting his unreadable black. Slowly, Ashley took the remaining steps and stopped in front of him. J.D.'s hand reached out and smoothed over the crown of her head, stroking the silky mane with unsteady fingers. Slowly his hands settled on her shoulders and he pulled her against him, lowering his head to hers to kiss her with total absorption and the intensity of a man saying good-bye forever. Tears poured down Ashley's pale face and she held him tightly. When he released her mouth, he buried his face against her hair.

"I could have loved you," he breathed against her ear in a tortured whisper. "God, how I could have loved you."

He tore himself from her arms and left the room without a backward glance. The two women stood frozen, hearing the thud of boot steps on the kitchen linoleum before the slamming door echoed through the house and back to them.

Magda released a pent-up breath, her wondering green gaze going to Ashley's bereft, tear-streaked face.

"My word, if a man kissed me like that, I'm not sure I could leave him!"

"I don't want to," Ashley sobbed, "but this isn't just about love. He has to learn to trust me.

He doesn't really believe that I love him and that I'll come back.''

Magda put an arm around Ashley's shoulders and opened the door.

''Well, dear, an hour ago I didn't think you'd be back either. But now I'm not so sure.''

Ashley cried all the way to Boise and boarded the plane to New York awash in grief and tears.

TEN

J.D. tipped his head back and glared up at the leaden sky. It was going to snow again. Those same skies had dropped enough snow on Idaho in the last two months to challenge any record ever set by Alaska. If the weather kept this up, he'd still be shoveling snow in July!

The truck bed he was riding in jolted over a hillock in the rough pasture and J.D. staggered, catching himself before throwing Ace a killing glare through the pickup's rear window.

"Watch it!" he roared. Ace shrugged and lifted a gloved hand in apology and faced forward again.

J.D. snipped the twine holding another hay bale and shoved it off over the lowered tailgate of the slow-moving truck. There was already a string of broken bales and scattered hay spread out in an uneven line across the Home Pasture. White-faced cattle stood with their noses buried in the fragrant dried alfalfa, their curly thick coats making bright reddish-brown splotches of color against the background of white snow and green hay. Several cows and steers plodded close behind the tailgate, waiting for J.D. to kick off another bale.

He cut the last bale free and shoved it off the truck before striding forward and pounding a gloved fist on the roof of the cab. Ace looked back and slowed to a stop, and J.D. jumped over the wheel well to climb quickly into the passenger side of the truck.

"Damn! It's cold out there!" he growled, and pushed the truck's heater levers to high.

"Yup," agreed Ace. "Sure is. And from the looks of that sky, this weather ain't gonna break anytime soon."

J.D. grunted in acknowledgment and lit a cigarette, staring silently out the side window while Ace turned the truck and drove slowly across the uneven pasture back to the barns.

Fat white snowflakes were drifting earthward by the time Ace parked the truck and the two slid out of the cab.

"Hey, boss, George and Bud and I are goin' into town tonight to the Blue Cougar, why don't you come along?"

Ace could see the refusal on J.D.'s hard face

and before he could voice it, the foreman hurried into speech.

"It'll be good for you, J.D. You ain't been off this place since Ashley—well, since Christmas."

"You don't need to tiptoe around it, Ace. I haven't been to town on Saturday night since Ashley left and you think it's because of her!" J.D. snarled, glaring at the older man.

"I don't meant to beat around the bush, J.D., but you've gotta admit, you're a shade touchy when anyone mentions the lady!"

"So what?" J.D. demanded.

"So nothin'!" Ace shot back. "But any darn fool knows the best remedy for what ails you is a shot of good whiskey and another woman!"

"Huh!" J.D. snorted. "Any fool knows you shouldn't get involved with a *woman* in the first place!"

"Yeah, well, maybe so. But if you already *have*, the best thing you can do is to forget her with another woman!"

"That's the stupidest thing I ever heard!"

"Well, stupid or not, it sure as hell beats sittin' home in that empty house night after night, drinkin' all by yourself!"

J.D. didn't answer, but Ace met his narrow-eyed stare without blinking. Finally, the older man broke the stubborn silence.

"If you change your mind, you're welcome to ride in with us. Or come on in later, if you want to."

J.D. nodded curtly, tugged his Stetson lower, and stepped out of the shelter of the barn, hunching his shoulders against the cold, snowfilled wind as he walked alone toward the dark ranchhouse.

"Damn fool!" Ace muttered, watching him go. "Reckon he's gonna' waste another Saturday night sittin' up there all alone, drinkin' and thinkin' about Ashley!"

Still muttering to himself, he pulled his own hat lower and set off across the cold lot toward his small bungalow.

J.D. pushed open the kitchen door and paused on the threshold. The room was dark. No fragrant aromas of cooking filled the empty kitchen, no ponytailed woman with soft skin, silky hair, and gold eyes glowing with welcome stood at the stove.

Damn her! He steeled himself against the now familiar pain that hit him every time he entered the kitchen. Memories filled every room in the house. He couldn't sit in his big leather recliner without remembering Ashley perched on the arm and teasing him. Upstairs in his room, sleep eluded him without Ashley's soft warmth curved against him in the old oak bed.

He bit off an oath and stamped across the kitchen and up the stairs to the bathroom and a hot shower. By nine o'clock, J.D. had eaten a tasteless frozen dinner, watched the news on television without really hearing it, stared at the same page of a Louis L'Amour novel for an hour without reading a word, and let thirty minutes of an Alan Ladd western movie run without seeing a single scene.

The silence pressed down around him. Maybe Ace was right. Maybe it was time he spent a night out with the boys. It damn sure wasn't doing him any good sitting around here pining away over a woman he'd never see again.

He pushed out of the recliner with sudden decision, shrugged into his jacket, pulled on his hat and left the house.

The Blue Cougar was hot and smokey after the cold, clear night air outside. J.D. stepped through the doorway and paused, black gaze searching the noisy, crowded room.

"J.D.! Hey, J.D.!"

Ace's bellow carried easily to J.D.'s ears over the music and laughter. He was sitting at a table against the far wall with Bud and George and J.D. wound his way through the crowd to join them, skirting packed tables and laughing patrons.

Ace gave him a wide grin and pulled out a chair.

"Have a seat, boss. Glad you could make it."

"What can I get you, J.D.?"

"Beer," J.D. answered the curvy, black-haired waitress. She gave him an appreciative smile and he forced himself to smile back.

Ace nudged him when she turned her back and hurried off.

"She likes you."

"What makes you think that?"

"Did you see the way she smiled at you? Yessir, she likes you, all right. Play your cards right, you could be takin' her home tonight!"

"What makes you think I want to take her home?" J.D. asked, irritated.

"Why not?" Ace demanded, insulted that J.D. wasn't impressed with the woman.

J.D. didn't answer because the waitress was returning with his beer.

"Hey, Chrissie," Bud said, grinning at the young woman. "How about savin' a dance for me later?"

"Sure, Bud," she smiled at the young cowboy and her gaze flicked back to J.D.'s noncommital face. "My shift ends at eleven."

J.D. didn't acknowledge the broad hint and Chrissie hurried away to answer a call for drinks from another table.

"So why aren't you interested?" Ace pressed J.D. for an answer when the brunette was out of earshot. "That's one nice lookin' woman!"

"Back off, Ace," J.D. growled. "I'm here, aren't I? I'm not sitting at home."

"Yeah, but—"

"You're worse than an old woman! You're not my mother, for god's sake! Now drop it!"

Ace shrugged and downed a healthy swig of foamy beer. Bud and George were used to Ace haranguing J.D. and their boss growling back so they ignored the two. The four spent the next hour drinking beer, smoking fat black cigars and arguing the merits of quarterhorses versus George's beloved appaloosas.

It was barely past eleven o'clock when J.D. looked up to see Chrissie nearing their table. She smiled invitingly at him and he smiled politely back, a mere curving of his lips.

She stopped at his side, resting fingers tipped with long, scarlet-painted nails on his shoulder.

"I'm off work, guys. Anybody here feel like dancing?"

Bud started eagerly to his feet but Ace kicked his shin, hard. He yelped with pain and stumbled forward, bumping the table and Chrissie at the same time.

Chrissie gave a shriek of surprise and tumbled backward into J.D.'s lap. His arms caught her, wrapping around her curvy shape in a quick, reflexive action. She lay in his arms, laughing up at him, one hand clutching his shoulder.

As luck would have it, Blake and Joanne had just entered the Blue Cougar and were searching the room for an empty table. They were threading their way through the crowded room, pausing to chat and say hello to friends when a disturbance at a nearby table caught their attention.

"J.D.!"

He looked up to find Joanne staring at him, indignation and outrage coloring her expressive face. Behind her, Blake watched the scene with amusement in his slate-grey eyes.

Joanne had been his friend for years but J.D. had had all he could take of meddling friends. Ace had used up the last of his patience much earlier.

Her indignation at finding the black-haired young woman lolling in his lap was plain to see. J.D. didn't wait to hear the lecture that he was sure was trembling on her lips. An imp of perverseness made him pull Chrissie closer while he smiled insolently up at Joanne.

"Evenin', Joanne, Blake. You know Chrissie, don't you?" He stood up in one easy motion, setting the young woman on her feet but keeping his arm around her shoulders and pulling her close against him. "You'll have to excuse us, we were just about to dance."

And with that, he turned and walked away from them, pulling the willing Chrissie along behind him, leaving Joanne to stare after them with narrowed eyes.

"Ace Langan!" She whirled to fix the older man with a furious glare. "What have you been up to?"

He looked up at her and spread his hands wide with an innocent air.

"Nothin'! Nothin' at all, Joanne! You know me—I never meddle!"

"Hah! That's the biggest lie you've ever told! What is J.D. doing with Chrissie Kendricks?"

"Dancin'. That's all, Joanne, just dancin'." Ace waved a hand at the dance floor, inviting Joanne to see for herself, his face all injured innocence.

Joanne stared at the crowded dance floor where the black-haired young woman was plastered against J.D.'s chest.

"You haven't been in for awhile, J.D.," Chrissie was saying, snuggling closer against his broad chest. J.D. McCullough wasn't a regular patron at the Blue Cougar, but before Christmas, Chrissie had seen him every now and then and been attracted to his dark good looks and well-built body. Though she'd tried to flirt with him, he'd never responded until now.

"No," J.D. agreed, wondering why her cuddling against him only aroused a mild irritation. He tightened his arms a fraction and dropped his cheek against her temple. "I've been busy—the weather's been lousy."

"Yes, I know," she answered sympathetically, delighted with his overtures. She wiggled, moving her breasts seductively against his chest. "I'm so sick of winter I could die! Wouldn't you just love to fly off to Mexico and lie in the sun for a week?"

"Yeah," he answered noncommittally, restraining a grimace at the sprayed stiffness of her hair beneath his cheek. The sweet smell of her perfume was cloying and overwhelming instead of seductive and he restrained an urge to push her away and drag in a lungful of clear air.

Chrissie ran her fingers over his nape and into his hair and J.D.'s whole body stiffened with rejection. He glanced down at the woman he held in his arms and knew with awful clarity that it was no use.

She was warm. She was willing. She had generous curves in all the right places. But she wasn't Ashley. J.D. knew it wouldn't work. Now all he had to do was figure out how he was going to tell Chrissie that.

Fortunately for J.D., Chrissie Kendricks was no fool. She knew when a man was responding and when he wasn't. She'd had her heart broken a few times and recognized all the signs in the tall, broad-shouldered man who held her in his arms. Added to her experience was the gossip making the rounds about the elusive rancher and Joanne Kleeman's model friend from New York. Chrissie eased back in his arms, putting a spare two inches between their bodies and tilting her head back to search his face.

"Tell me, J.D.," she said with sympathetic warmth. "Are you dancing with me to prove something to yourself or to get Ace and Joanne off your back?"

Startled, J.D. started to deny any duplicity but the empathy on her round face made him tell her the truth.

"A little of both," he admitted. "Are you upset?"

"No, not at all," she responded promptly. "It's hard enough having a broken heart without having well-meaning friends driving you crazy, too."

"I don't have a broken heart," J.D. denied vehemently, frowning down at her.

"Okay, okay, so you don't have a broken heart." She smiled at him. "Maybe it's not broken, maybe it's just bent a little?"

Startled, he stared at her for a moment before shrugging, a small smile lifting the corner of his mouth.

"Maybe."

She laughed and patted one broad shoulder in a friendly, comforting gesture.

"Don't feel like the Lone Ranger, fella, it happens to the best of us sometimes. Take me, for example. I've fallen in and out of love a couple dozen times and had my poor heart shattered at least a dozen of those times. Frankly, my friend, love can be the pits!"

J.D. laughed out loud, the first genuine laugh he'd uttered since Ashley walked out of his house.

"You want some advice, friend?"

J.D. stared at her for a long silent moment. He got daily rations of advice from Ace. He doubted she had anything new to tell him.

"Go after her," the brunette continued, ignoring his silence. "In my experience, if she's worth breaking your heart over, she's probably worth putting out a little effort."

"I can't go after her," he said, slightly amazed that he was having this intensely personal conversation with a woman he hardly knew.

"Why not?"

"Because it wouldn't do any good."

"Why not?"

"Because she wouldn't come back with me—she's working."

"So? Wait till she's done working and then kidnap her if she won't come back."

"It wouldn't work. She'd just leave again as soon as I turned my back. She has *contracts*," he bit out the word with loathing.

"Well," Chrissie said reasonably. "Wait until she finishes her contracts and then go and kidnap her and drag her back."

"I wouldn't need to drag her back by then—she said she'd come back after her contract work is finished."

Chrissie looked at him as if he were slightly demented.

"Well then, what's the big deal? If she's coming back when she's finished working, why are you so down in the dumps over this whole thing?"

"Because if she loved me, she'd forget the contracts and be here with me now."

"If that isn't just like a man!" Chrissie exclaimed, shaking her head in disgust. "Did it ever occur to you that contracts are important to women? After all, marriage is a contract, too! How would you feel if you married her and she decided to walk out on *your* contract?"

J.D. stared at her, nonplussed.

"I never thought of it that way," he said slowly.

"Men!" The brunette rolled her eyes in disgust. Her gaze went past his shoulder to find Joanne glaring at her from where she sat beside Blake. "Your friend doesn't look pleased with you."

"Which friend?" J.D. asked, busily mulling over her earlier comments.

"Joanne."

J.D.'s dark gaze followed hers and found Joanne, her fair skin flushed with anger, blue eyes fuming as she stared at him. He winced and looked ruefully down into Chrissie's amused eyes.

"She doesn't look too happy, does she?" he commented.

"Nope."

The three-piece band chose that moment to take a ten minute break and J.D. walked Chrissie back to his table.

"Thanks for the dance, J.D.," she smiled up at him and touched his arm. "I doubt it'll happen, but if things don't work out for you, look me up."

J.D. smiled back, somehow soothed by her friendly concern and interest.

Before he could respond, she turned and pulled Bud to his feet.

"Come on, cowboy, we're playing a game of pool." And with that, she drug a willing Bud off toward the pool tables, leaving J.D. to cope with Ace and Joanne by himself.

Ace was beaming his approval of J.D.'s actions.

But Joanne lost no time in telling him exactly how she felt about his dancing with the cute little darkhaired waitress.

She plunked herself down in the chair next to him and planted her folded arms atop the table.

"J.D. McCullough, just what do you think you're doing?" she demanded, fixing him with accusing blue eyes.

"Drinking my beer and minding my own business," he said pointedly, tilting the longnecked amber bottle to his lips.

"Hah!" she snorted disbelievingly. "You weren't drinking beer a few minutes ago when you had Chrissie Kendricks plastered all over you on the dance floor!"

J.D. sighed and returned the bottle to the tabletop.

"She wasn't plastered all over me," he began but Joanne interrupted him.

"It certainly looked like it from where I was sitting! I just don't understand you, J.D.! How you can fool around with someone else when you have Ashley is beyond——"

"I don't have Ashley," J.D. interrupted grimly, his features hardening, dark eyes meeting Joanne's accusing blue eyes with equal stubbornness.

"You will have in another few months!"

"Sure I will!" J.D.'s voice was bitter. "You really think she'll come back here to live on a ranch in Idaho after she's been to New York? The city can offer her things I can't possibly compete with, and you know it. Once she's had a chance to compare what I can give her with the glamorous life she lives in New York, there's no way she'll be back."

Joanne's eyes filled with tears and she reached out to touch his arm.

"That's not true, J.D., she loves you. I know she does. She wants a life with you. You're what's important to her, not some illusion of glamour."

"Yeah, right." J.D. didn't believe her. But oh, god, how he wished he could!

Abruptly, he pulled his arm away from her comforting touch. He'd had all he could take of well-meaning friends.

"Good night, Joanne, Ace."

The two left sitting at the table watched helplessly while he shouldered his way through the crowd and disappeared through the door and into the night. Alone.

The weeks dragged on. Every now and then J.D. joined Ace and the boys at the Blue Cougar on a Saturday night but he didn't dance again. Chrissie teased him gently and he appreciated her concern, but he just wasn't interested.

Late one Saturday near midnight, he'd worked his way through a quarter of a bottle of good whiskey while he stared unseeingly at a movie. The phone rang shrilly in the kitchen, jarring him out of his half-dreams. He pushed the recliner upright and padded in stocking feet into the kitchen. Three days growth of beard shadowed his face and he'd been too tired when he came in to even shower so his worn jeans were stiff with mud below the knees, his wool flannel shirt carried its share of small splatters, too.

"Hello," he growled into the receiver. No one answered. Impatiently, he spoke again. "Hello."

"Hello, J.D."

Ashley's faintly husky voice carried softly over the phone lines and caused his knees to buckle. He braced one hand against the wall by the phone and leaned his forehead against his arm.

"Ashley." His own voice held all the agony and longing of the long weeks apart.

Ashley almost cried with relief. At least he hadn't hung up on her.

"How are you?" she managed to get out, twisting the phone cord nervously in her fingers.

"How am I?" he repeated blankly, still numb with shock and unable to lie to her. "Not good. I've been better. How about you?"

"Not good. I've been better, too," she replied.

"Where are you?" he asked, beginning to recover his balance, starting to remember all the differences that separated them.

"I'm in Barbados."

"Barbados! That's a hell of a long ways away from New York!" *And Idaho,* he added silently.

"Yes, I know," Ashley answered, his deep

voice conjuring up mental pictures of his dark face and eyes and the thick black hair that felt like rough silk against her fingers. She closed her eyes, visualizing his tall, broad-shouldered body, and the frown that she was sure was pulling his dark brows together, drawing creases between them that she longed to smooth away with her fingertips.

"What are you doing there?"

"Modeling bathing suits and beachwear, hats, cover-ups, sandals, that sort of thing."

"Oh."

"J.D.," she whispered, all pretense dissolving, tears making her voice waver, "I miss you so much!"

"God, honey," he said achingly, his eyes squeezing shut with longing and pain. "I miss you, too. Come home, baby. Right now. Catch the next plane out—I'll pick you up."

"There's nothing I'd rather do! But I can't. Not yet." She was crying now, her words interrupted by sobs.

"Why not?" he demanded, pain making his voice rough.

"You know why not. I gave my word when I signed those contracts. I can't back out of them."

"Yeah," J.D. sighed in defeat. "I reckon we're right back where we started. You won't give up your world and I won't give up mine. Stalemate."

"Not forever, J.D. I only have a couple of months left, and then . . ."

"Don't say it, honey. We might as well face the truth. You won't be able to settle for a dull life with me in my world and I won't join you in yours. It's over." His voice was grim.

"No, no, J.D., that's not how it is at all!" Ashley protested, tears thickening her voice.

"Yes it is, baby. You just don't want to admit it. Go back to your own world, honey, and leave me alone in mine."

Ashley could hardly bear the remote, grim finality in his beloved voice.

"I love you, J.D.," she managed to get out.

"I love you, too, baby."

The line went dead and he stared at the receiver in his hand for one long moment before dropping it on the countertop. He slammed one fist against the wall, never noticing the pain in his cut hand as he dropped his face against his bent arm while unfamiliar tears rolled down his cheeks.

ELEVEN

"J.D.'s impossible, Ashley!" Joanne complained in frustration. "Ever since you left he's been like an old grizzly bear forced out of hibernation! He doesn't even smile for Cassie any more and he's always adored her. And if I mention your name, he snarls at me."

Ashley sighed. In the three months since she'd left Idaho, she'd lived for these twice weekly telephone calls to Joanne and news of J.D. They were her only contact with him for she was determined not to talk to him again until she could do so in person. She was miserable and the only consolation was that J.D. seemed just as miserable.

"I miss him so much I can hardly stand it," she told Joanne, curling the telephone cord around her index finger, staring unseeing at the Victorian elegance of her bedroom.

"Do you think you'll be finished by the end of April?" Joanne asked.

"I'm not sure—I may have to fly to L.A.; if I do, I won't be done until the sixth of May," Ashley said reluctantly. She'd give anything if she could give in and fly back to Idaho but her ingrained sense of responsibility refused to let her renege on her contracts.

"Has Maggie accepted that you're not going to be modeling anymore?"

"Yes." An affectionate smile lifted the sad droop of Ashley's mouth. "I'm not sure, but I think she started accepting it when she saw J.D. kiss me good-bye. She told me that if anyone ever kissed her like that, she might think of leaving the city for the wilds of Idaho, too!"

"Really?" Joanne laughed with surprise. "Can't you just see it? Maggie in jeans and boots cleaning out horse stalls?!"

Ashley chuckled fondly.

"Not really. But she says she'll come to Idaho and visit me and J.D. when the babies arrive."

"I hope you can get close enough to get babies!" Joanne said with a snort. "The way he's snarling at everything that gets within ten feet of him lately, I wouldn't bet on it!"

Ashley refused to listen to the little worried voice in her head that echoed Joanne's concern.

"I refuse to consider that he won't let me come back," she said firmly, pushing doubt and apprehension firmly behind her. "Even if he picks me up and throws me bodily off the ranch, I'll hang around and slowly but surely wear him down. He'll get so sick of seeing me, sooner or later he'll give in!"

"I hope so," but Joanne sounded doubtful. "Even Ace is threatening to quit, J.D.'s been so hard to live around."

She'd never told Ashley about seeing J.D. in the Blue Cougar with Chrissie. She refused to believe that he wasn't faithful; J.D. gave every impression of being a one-woman man. Why else would he be so incredibly impossible if he wasn't pining away for Ashley?

Ashley hung up the phone and forced herself to get out of bed. It was only five-thirty in the morning, but the sun already lit the room through the lowered shades. It was a lovely hotel room in an exotic, beautiful setting but she would have traded it for Idaho snow and J.D. in a heartbeat.

"Ashley Tierney! Didn't you sleep at all last night!"

The makeup technician frowned at her in disgust, eyeing the pale lavendar circles etched beneath the gold eyes.

"Sorry, Gary," Ashley said with an apologetic smile. "I tried, but I just couldn't fall asleep."

Gary propped a hand on one hip and tilted his head quizzically.

"Hmmmm," he trailed a soft, fat makeup brush in little parentheses beside her mouth. "Could it be our lady has man problems?"

Ashley gave him a wry grin.

"Hmmmm," she parroted. "Could be."

"Well, I'll be damned!" The lanky body straightened in surprise, his mouth falling open. "It's about time! Who is he? Do I know him?"

Ashley shook her head and soft curls escaped from the exquisite hairdo the beautician had just completed.

"Hey! Cut that out!" Teresa descended on her with combs and hairpins and quickly secured the falling hair.

"Be kind to her, Tessie," Gary said with a wide grin. "Our Ashley has man trouble."

Teresa's brown eyes opened wide with astonishment.

"What? Not our Ashley! Who is he? What's his name? Do I know him?"

Teased out of her sadness, Ashley couldn't help but laugh at the two whom she'd often worked with over the last five years.

She held up her fingers and ticked off her answers.

"Yes, *your* Ashley. His name is J.D. McCullough, and no, you don't know him."

More questions trembled on Teresa's lips but

the photographer interrupted them, impatiently demanding why Ashley wasn't ready, and Gary quickly worked his magic with his pots and lotions.

Just as he whisked the all-enveloping cape away from her shoulders, he whispered in her ear.

"Whoever he is, he better stop causing you sleepless nights or Tessie and I will have his head on a pike!"

Ashley laughed, cheered by her friend's concern, and went to work.

The sixth of May arrived at long last. Ashley flew to Boise and drove north to Joanne's home. It was midafternoon by the time she'd showered, carefully applied makeup, donned the dress she'd spent two weeks shopping for in New York, and drove to the Lazy M. It was unseasonably warm for early May, the thermometer hovered at seventy-two degrees but snow still lingered on the mountaintops and in shadowed, sheltered places deep beneath stands of pines.

J.D.'s mudspattered silver pickup was parked with several other trucks in front of the big barn and Ashley drove her rental car past the house and braked next to it. She took one last nervous look in the mirror to check her makeup and hair before getting out of the car. A cloud of dust drifted up from the corrals behind the barn and the shouts of men mixed with the angry neighing of horses.

She pressed a nervous hand to her midriff,

smoothing damp palms down the slim green skirt of the halter dress, and took three deep, calming breaths to settle the butterflies in her stomach. She'd thought about little else but this moment for the last four months and now that it was here, she was terrified.

What if he doesn't want me anymore? What if he meant it when he told me he wouldn't take me back?

There was no way to know the answers without facing him. She squared her shoulders, lifted her chin and walked around the barn and into full view of the dozen or so men perched on the corral rails, shouting and yelling encouragement as a cowboy was pitched back and forth on a twisting, spinning, snorting bronc inside the dusty corral. Ashley paused, narrowing her lashes in an attempt to locate J.D. among the spurred, booted cowboys in Levis and Stetsons. Before she could locate him, Nate Tucker spotted her and elbowed the man at his side.

"I'll be damned," he whistled between his teeth. "Isn't that—?"

Ed Thorson stared hard before a wide grin split his broad face.

"That's the woman from back East that stayed with J.D. last Christmas! I wonder what she's doing here?"

J.D. heard the buzz of interest that stirred among the men on the corral fence and looked up from the lariat in his hands. They were all staring, gaping at something behind him. With little interest, he glanced over his left shoulder and froze.

Ashley stood some fifty yards behind him, her golden gaze searching the men sitting on the corral rails. From the top of her shiny head to the ridiculous, strappy little green-heeled sandals on her feet, she was gloriously, beautifully female. An emerald-green halter dress clung to high, firm breasts and J.D. wondered achingly if she was wearing anything under the clinging fabric. The halter left her shoulders and arms bare and the skirt clung faithfully to her hips and thighs before ending just above her knees. Gold bangle bracelets clinked as she lifted one hand to shade her eyes against the sunlight.

He dropped the lariat and swung lithely down from the corral. Ashley spotted him the moment he swung away from the top rail of the corral, her throat going dry at the sight of him. He wore a blue chambray shirt, left unbuttoned in the afternoon heat. Leather chaps covered his long legs. The pale scarred leather bracketed and defined the blatant maleness beneath his silver belt buckle. The brim of the Stetson threw his hard face into shadow, but even at this distance she could see that the black eyes were expressionless, his face remote and cool.

You knew this wasn't going to be easy, she told

herself sternly. *Don't be such a ninny! Talk to him! Get it over with!*

"Hello, J.D." Her voice came out husky and just the tiniest bit shaky.

Her words traveled up J.D.'s spine and rippled through his gut, sending waves of fierce wanting throughout his hard body. But no reaction moved across his expressionless face.

"Hello, Ashley," he said evenly, his deep voice calm and cool. "What are you doing here?"

Ashley felt a small bit of relief. At least he was going to talk to her before he threw her off his ranch.

"I finished my last shoot," she said softly, watching him carefully for his reaction.

"Oh yeah?" His voice displayed no interest.

"I gave up my apartment," she went on.

He didn't respond. He just stood there, watching her, fingers splayed over his hips as if waiting patiently for her to leave. Ashley started to lose her nervousness, and her patience.

"I packed all my belongings and had them shipped here," she continued. He still didn't answer. Her fingers curled into fists.

"You asked me to marry you, J.D. McCullough, and I'm not letting you off the hook!" She planted her fists on her hips and glared at him, her golden eyes fired with anger. "I'll sue for breach of promise! I'll tell Aunt Maggie and Ace I'm pregnant and they'll hold the shotgun!"

He started striding toward her, purposefully, inexorably.

Ashley stopped yelling at him and eyed him uncertainly.

"Are you?" he demanded in a hard voice.

"Are I what?" she asked, standing her ground in spite of his threatening approach.

"Are you pregnant?" he asked, only three strides away from her now.

"No," she said nervously. "J.D., what are you—"

Her voice was cut off by his mouth descending on hers with punishing force, his arms wrapping around her to bind her tightly against him. He bent his knees and lifted her off the ground without moving his mouth from hers. Ashley wound her arms around his neck and kissed him back just as fiercely, tears running down her flushed face.

"I love you," she murmured against his mouth. "Love you, love—"

His big body jerked in reaction, his mouth desperately hungry as it ravaged hers.

Heated moments passed before he ripped his mouth from hers and glared down at her, his black eyes hot.

"Damn you, you little witch!"

Dazed, Ashley could only look up at him in bewilderment.

He bent and butted a broad shoulder into her midriff, lifting her easily to toss her over his shoulder. A cheer of male approval and encouragement went up from the avidly staring cowboys lining the corral.

"Attaboy, J.D.!"

"Yahoo, cowboy! Way to go!"

The hoots and catcalls followed them around the corner of the barn. Ashley's soft middle jolted against the rock-hard muscles of his shoulder and she winced, the blood rushing to her head to flush her face a hot pink.

"J.D.! Put me down! What do you think you're doing?!" She struggled and tried to kick him, but he locked an arm across her knees and controlled her feet with his other hand. She pounded small fists against his back but he ignored her, his long strides eating up the distance to the ranch house with ease.

He strode across the porch, through the front door, and up the stairway. Ashley's thick fall of hair swung over her eyes, but she recognized the carpet in his bedroom before he dumped her on her back on the broad oak bedstead and settled his weight on top of her. His hat went spinning across the room and his hard hands pinned her wrists beside her head.

"Now," he said with a deceptive calmness that belied the fierce black eyes, "tell me that again."

"Tell you what?" she said belligerently, twisting her hands in a useless effort to pull her wrists free. "Let go of me, you Neanderthal! You can't just throw me over your shoulder and haul me off to your cave!''

Her twisting slid the green dress higher, exposing the pale skin of her upper thigh and the lacy garters that held up her silk stockings. He glanced down and bit off an oath. The black gaze returned to hers, a black fire flaring up in his eyes. She froze, trapped by that mesmerizing gaze. He transferred her wrists to one hand above her head and without preliminaries, laid his palm against the bare skin of her thigh, shoving the green skirt up to her hips. In one easy move, he wedged her legs apart and settled between her thighs, openly aroused. The rough denim and slick leather chaps were cool against her soft, bare skin.

''Tell me,'' he said thickly. ''Say my name and tell me you love me.''

He looked down into her golden eyes and Ashley saw through the raw, angry hunger to his heart-wrenching need. The tension fled her body and she went soft and boneless beneath him.

''J.D.'' she breathed huskily. ''I love you.''

''I never thought I'd hear you say that,'' he growled and caught her chin in a hard hand. ''How long are you staying this time?''

''Forever.''

''You'd have hell to pay getting away any sooner, woman.'' He bucked his hips against her and she gasped as her body automatically returned the motion. "It'll be days before I even let you out of this bedroom."

Ashley tried to hang onto her fast-disappearing sanity and forced her eyes wide to look up into his hard face.

"Now, you tell me," she demanded softly.

"Tell you what?" he asked.

"Say my name and tell me you love me," she held her breath and waited. *Would he admit it? Did he love her?*

He was silent for a long moment, his black gaze drifting with slow strokes over her face.

"Ashley," he managed to get out hoarsely. "I love you. I'm completely worthless without you. I don't eat; I can't sleep. I tried to get drunk to forget you and even that didn't work. If you ever go away again, I'll follow you to the ends of the earth and drag you back. I'm never going through this again!"

Tears were raining down her face.

"Oh, J.D.," she sobbed. "I feel exactly the same."

His gentle fingers smoothed away the dampness, followed by warm lips that cherished every inch of her face.

Down at the corral, the exhausted bronc finally gave in and was led away. Ace listened to Nate and Ed tell him about J.D.'s visitor, a broad grin spreading across his weathered face.

"Yessir," he told the two envious cowboys. "I

knew she'd be back, never doubted it! Women just naturally love J.D. McCullough. It was only a matter of time before he let one of them catch him. Smart boy, that J.D. And the little lady sure can cook!''

And in the big old bed where McCulloughs had been making babies for at least a hundred years, the last thing on J.D.'s mind was the little lady's cooking.

_____ EPILOGUE _____

"Magda, have you seen Ashley?"

Maggie turned away from the laughing, glittering group of men and women she was chatting with and smiled up at J.D.

"Not in the last few minutes. Have you lost her?"

"Good God, I hope not," he said with feeling.

Maggie ran a warmly approving glance over Ashley's tall, broad-shouldered husband of one year before searching the noisy crowd that filled her Manhattan apartment. Most of the people present were not only her friends but her niece's as well, gathered to congratulate Ashley and celebrate her success as an illustrator and the resulting coveted publisher's award for her last book.

"It's a bit smokey in here," Maggie commented. "She may have stepped out on the balcony for a breath of fresh air."

"Thanks, Maggie, I'll look out there."

Maggie's gaze followed his lithe figure in tailored evening clothes as he threaded his way through the throng and disappeared through the French doors that opened onto the apartment's balcony.

Ashley leaned against the balustrade and looked out over the lights of New York City spread out below her. The view was breathtaking, the May evening cooled with a faint breeze that lifted the heavy fall of hair away from her cheeks.

"Hello, beautiful. What are you doing out here all alone?"

The deep, amused voice was a welcome interruption to her thoughts and she turned to find J.D. standing just outside the French doors that led to Magda's apartment. He leaned negligently against the wall, one broad shoulder resting against the rough grey stone. Ashley's warm gaze ran lovingly over him. Formal wear suited him, she thought. He wore the black tuxedo with its glistening white, tucked-front shirt with the same easy aplomb as he did his workday boots and tight, faded jeans.

He pushed away from the wall and crossed the balcony to take her in his arms.

"There are too many people around," he growled softly, smiling down at her before his mouth closed over hers. When at last he lifted his black head, she was breathless, her lips softly swollen from the warm, wet pressure of his. He hugged her closer, molding her soft curves to the long line of his body, kissing the crown of her head before resting his chin against the silky curls. "Uhmmmm, that's much better," he murmured.

Ashley smiled against his throat, breathing in the beloved scents of aftershave, cigarettes, and pure male that was J.D.

"Are you having a good time?" she asked, snuggling closer against his warm body.

"Sure. Are you?"

"Yes, I'm having a lovely time." She tilted her head back to look up into his face. "I really appreciate your coming to New York with me, J.D. Receiving the award for my illustrations wouldn't have meant nearly as much without you here to share it."

"I'm glad, honey." His voice was husky with emotion. She tapped a deep well of feeling in him that no one else had ever touched. He offered a silent prayer of thanks that she belonged to him.

"I'm glad we're going home tomorrow, though," she continued, her voice muffled against his throat. This afternoon the doctor had confirmed what she had suspected for the last two weeks and she wanted to be in their own big oak bed in Idaho when she told him her news. She was faintly apprehensive about what his response would be to her announcement.

"What?" J.D. exclaimed in mock surprise. "Don't tell me you've had enough of the theatre, museums, and those marathon shopping expeditions with your aunt?"

"Oh, stop teasing me!" Ashley chuckled. "You men! You never understand that women love to go shopping!"

"Oh, I understand shopping," he replied. "What I don't understand is shopping all day, every day, for three days!"

"I didn't hear you objecting last night when I wore that new red silk teddy that I spent three hours searching for yesterday!"

"Well, now that you mention it," he said thoughtfully, "maybe there is some value to those shopping expeditions. I sure do love the way you look in that little lace and silk thing!"

Ashley laughed and nipped him gently.

"Ouch! Actually," he continued, "I like you better in nothing at all." He slid one hand up her back where the clinging black evening gown left her skin bare nearly to her waist. "Why don't you and I say good night to your aunt," he said huskily. "Suddenly, I'm awfully tired—I think we should go to bed."

Ashley's eyes turned dark and lambent as he stroked her, and her mouth went dry at the desire that flared hotly in his eyes.

"Yes, let's," she managed to get out.

*   *   *

Two days later, Ashley sat crosslegged in the center of the big oak bed and watched J.D. rubbing his hair dry with a towel. Another towel was slung around his hips, the terry cloth starkly white against tanned skin and the black curls that arrowed downward below his navel.

He finished drying his hair and tossed the damp towel over the doorknob before turning to catch Ashley unabashedly staring at him. A knowing grin curved the line of his mouth upward.

"Enjoying the view?" he drawled teasingly.

"Very much," she answered promptly, but her answering smile quickly faded and she watched him with solemn gold eyes while he stood in front of the dresser mirror and ran a brush through his hair.

J.D. tossed the brush back atop the dresser and crossed the room to drop down beside her on the bed.

"Honey," he said gently, stroking a calloused palm over the crown of her head, smoothing the thick, silky fall down her back, "you've had something on your mind for the last few days. Don't you think it's about time you told me so we can talk about it, whatever it is?"

She smiled tremulously up at him and nodded.

"Yes, it is time. I didn't tell you before because I wanted us to be home when I told you."

J.D.'s heart swelled with emotion at her use of the word home. Idaho was home to her now, not

New York. As for him, he knew that his home was wherever she was.

"Tell me, honey," he urged softly. "What is it? Is something wrong?"

"Not exactly, I mean—not exactly *wrong*. Remember when we decided that we would wait awhile to have children?"

"Sure, I remember. I wanted you to have time to get used to living on the ranch and for us to have some time together with just the two of us. Why? Have you changed your mind?"

"No, that is—well, *I* didn't change my mind. It's just that—well, J.D.—" She paused, catching his big hand in both of hers, and burst out, "I'm pregnant!"

J.D. stared at her, dumbstruck.

"Pregnant?" he repeated numbly. "Pregnant? You mean, we're going to have a baby?"

Ashley nodded, watching him anxiously.

"Are you angry? Honestly, J.D., I took the pill faithfully! The doctor said in a small percentage of cases, they just don't work and women can get pregnant no matter how careful they are." She peered into his blank face. "You are upset, aren't you?"

J.D. registered the worry in her voice and snapped back to earth.

"Oh, no! No, darlin', I'm not upset! I'm happy," he placed one large palm gently, tentatively over her flat stomach. "You're really pregnant?" he said with awe. "There's really a baby in there?"

He tugged open the short, green silk kimono she wore and bent to place a warm kiss against the slight curve of her stomach.

"Hello, baby," he whispered softly.

Ashley felt hot tears threaten and she didn't bother to blink them back. J.D. turned his cheek to lay against her soft skin and she slid her fingers gently over the hard bones of his cheeks and into the thick black hair.

"I want a little girl," he said, his eyes opening to look up at her. "A little girl with her mother's hair and eyes. A little girl just like you."

"And I want a little boy. A little boy with his father's hair and eyes," Ashley repeated, smiling mistily at the look of stunned happiness on her husband's handsome face.

"I'll settle for whatever God gives us. I just want this baby and its mommy to be healthy."

J.D. tumbled her over onto her back and made slow, exquisitely careful love to her.

And six months later, when the doctor delivered a boy and a girl—squalling, healthy twins—Ace Langan passed out cigars with pink and blue bands.

"Yessir," he told anyone who would listen to the proud, self-appointed grandfather. "I knew they'd have twins! Smart boy, that J.D.!"

SHARE THE FUN . . .
SHARE YOUR NEW-FOUND TREASURE!!

You don't want to let your new book out of your sight? That's okay. Your friends can get their own. Order below.

No. 1   ALWAYS by Catherine Sellers

Tall and handsome, Jared Sentrell, encountered the frightened Leza Colletti and his protective instincts took over. Even as she fell under the spell of his smokey gray eyes and electrifying kisses, Leza knew in her heart she must leave him.

No. 2   NO HIDING PLACE by Brooke Sinclair

Surely the pretty, blue-eyed blonde wasn't able to protect dark and sensual Dr. Matthew Stone from the terrorists chasing him . . . was she? Agent Corey Hamilton was that and more. And the *more* Matthew was intent on finding out about.

No. 3   SOUTHERN HOSPITALITY by Sally Falcon

Logan Herrington, a Yankee with an attitude, had a chip on his shoulder a mile high . . . and Tory Planchet, smart, sexy and bold, was just the one to knock it off. Logan was about to learn "southern hospitality" Tory-style!!

No. 4   WINTERFIRE by Lois Faye Dyer

What was beautiful, successful New York model, Ashley Tierney, doing on a ranch in Antelope, Idaho? Bewitched by her enchanting, lioness eyes, that's exactly what ruggedly handsome J.D. McCullough decided to find out.

Kismet Romances
Dept 790, P. O. Box 41820, Philadelphia, PA 19101-9828

Please send the books I've indicated below. Check or money order only— no cash, stamps or C.O.D.'s (PA residents, add 6% sales tax). I am enclosing $2.75 plus 75¢ handling fee for *each* book ordered.
    Total Amount enclosed: $_____.

____No. 1   ____ No. 2   ____ No. 3   ____ No. 4

Please Print:

Name_____

Address_____Apt. No._____

City/State_____ Zip_____

Allow four to six weeks for delivery. Quantities limited.

Kismet Romances has for sale a Mini Handi Light to help you when reading in bed, reading maps in the car or for emergencies where light is needed. Features an on/off switch; lightweight plastic housing and strong-hold clamp that attaches easily to books, car visor, shirt pocket etc. 11″ long. Requires 2 "AA" batteries (not included). If you would like to order, send $9.95 each to: Mini Handi Light Offer, P.O. Box 41820, Phila., PA 19101-9828. PA residents must add 6% sales tax. Please allow 8 weeks for delivery. Supplies are limited.